ONCE
WERE
COPS

KEN BRUEN

ONCE WERE COPS

St. Martin's Minotaur
New York

This is a work of fiction. All of the characters, organizations, and events portrayed in this novel are either products of the author's imagination or are used fictitiously.

www.minotaurbooks.com

Library of Congress Cataloging-in-Publication Data

Bruen, Ken.
    Once were cops / Ken Bruen. —1st St. Martin's Minotaur ed.
    p. cm.
  ISBN-13: 978-0-312-38440-1
  ISBN-10: 0-312-38440-8
  1. Police—New York (State)—New York—Fiction 2. Police brutality—Fiction. 3. Serial murderers—Fiction. 4. New York (N.Y.)—Fiction. I. Title.
PR6052.R785053 2008
823'.914—dc22

                              2008025096

First Edition: November 2008

10 9 8 7 6 5 4 3 2 1

For Robert Ward, true literary renegade and four kinds of friend
And Brian Lidenmouth . . . without whom this book wouldn't have been written
And Honora Finklstein, Susan Smiley, Gold Hearts

It takes a particular kind of psycho
to be a really effective cop.

—Graffiti on the wall of a restroom
in Lower Manhattan

ONCE
WERE
COPS

ONE

"WHERE DO I BEGIN?'

Wasn't that like a song?

And a pretty fucking bad one.

Like my story.

The old chestnut, *and how did what started out so good, go so freaking bad?*

The Yanks whine . . .

"Who you gonna call?"

God?

Do me a favor.

Whatever else is in this narrative, it ain't Him.

Unless He was seriously fucking with us.

Somebody was.

My name is Matthew Patrick O'Shea.

And you're thinking,

"Does it come any more Mick?"

Not a lot.

Course, everybody called me Shea.

Has a ring to it and the first thing I did in America, yeah, Shea Stadium.

Predictable.

Sure.

If only I'd stayed thus.

Right at the end, when the shite was coming from every direction, I'd have given a lot for a dose of me own predictability.

I grew up in Galway, the son of a Guard, and it was never for debate but that I'd follow in me old man's heavy shoes.

I HAVE THIS SPLIT PERSONALITY GIG GOING, TRULY, *good cop/bad cop*.

You'll notice the caps there, so you'll know I told you from the off.

Part of me has always wanted to be a decent human being, and being a cop seemed like a way I could make a difference. People like me, no shit, it's just the truth and I've always known how to get them to do so.

Nothing wrong with that.

Then there's the zoning, from the time I was a child, I'd go someplace in my mind, a cold place and it's like seeing the world through a fog or very heavy glass and what I most want is to do damage, biblical damage, it's beyond rage, more like a controlled fury that oh so careful watches, then strikes. I saw a cobra once on the TV and that hooded head, the poise and then the ferocious strike . . .

I never saw anything more beautiful in my life and I felt I was inside that hood. My mother used to say,

"Shea lives in another room."

A room covered in ice and fierceness.

My father said,

"Ah, he'll grow out if it."

He was so close . . . what I did was grow *into* it. I knew some bad stuff happened when I was zoned but I'd only barely recall it after. There was a priest in our parish, named Brennan, he liked me as I was one hell of a hurler.

Hurling is our national sport, a cross between hockey and murder.

I'd zone in games and some poor bastard would end up with forty stitches in his head.

Fr. Brennan liked to win, and our team never lost because he used to say,

"Let Shea loose."

He spoke to me one time and asked,

"How does that change happen, is it the adrenaline of the game?"

And I told him of the zoning, he looked worried, then said,

"Don't ever tell another soul about this, they'd lock you up."

Then he handed me a green rosary beads, it was a few weeks before Easter and the days were offering up rare moments of sunshine, as I took them. It was a lovely piece, gold cross, emerald beads and silver threads. The sun came flooding through the windows, catching the beads in a shaft of sheer translucence, and I felt a jolt of electricity that nearly knocked me off my feet.

Fr. Brennan said,

"You grip that beads when the shadows invade your mind and pray to our Holy Mother and all the saints to deliver you."

I did grip the beads like a vise when the shadows came creeping but didn't ask for help, I wanted something entirely different, a release from the pressure building in my head, and the longing for this sometimes had the beads cutting into the palms of my hands.

I felt like I'd been gloriously crucified.

It was such delicious agony.

I began to collect rosary beads but they had to be green, and I began to watch movies like a person possessed, cop movies especially.

Thing is, I always loved cop movies. Thing was, being a Guard didn't jell with the cop movies I watched.

I mean, do you really think you're going to see a movie titled:

The Guards?

Yeah, like that's going to happen.

First, the Guards don't carry guns.

Fuck that.

Right.

Saturday night, you're facing off against a drunk gang, you think a baton is going to disperse them.

Especially as the bastards were carrying.

And not sticks.

Like fuck.

I did me year.

Pounding the wet miserable streets of Galway, soaked to the skin, freezing me nuts off and thinking,

"Has to be something better than this."

Then my old man died, he'd been connected, to a politician. He'd gotten a drunk driving gig quashed and did some other stuff too.

The guy, Kearns, at the funeral, said to me,

"Anything you need, you call me."

I did.

Told him,

"I want a green card."

He had the eyes of a rat, and the smile of one too, he stretched back in his oh so expensive leather chair, asked,

"And why would you want to go to Amer-i-kay?"

Leaning on the word, playing with it, playing with me.

The bollix.

But I let him screw around, I wanted this and if it meant eating shite, give me the shovel.

He added,

"The whole world wants to come and live here, especially the Yanks, and you, you want to go the other direction?"

Story of my life.

I had me a temper, a bad one, hair trigger me mother said.

Mind you, she said a lot of stuff, most of it garbage.

I said,

"I'm still young, want to travel a bit."

Biting down on the anger I felt building, trying not to tell
him to go shove it. He said,

"Not as easy as it used to be."

Here we go, so I said,

"My old man, he kept files, I was thinking I should burn
them, what do you think?"

Got me green card.

And the green rosary beads.

My mother wept . . . buckets, course, the half bottle of dry
sherry she put away before lunch might have helped.

"And what will you do, *amac?*" Son.

I gave her me best smile, the one in me first communion
photo, said,

"I'll do the best I can."

We'd recently had Clinton on a visit and he was especially
impressed with our police force, that we didn't carry
guns. He helped put in place an exchange program
where twenty Guards would go to America and twenty
of their finest would come here. The Guards would be
sent all over the States, for that overall view. I knew
what I wanted and it wasn't some backwater down

south, I wanted the big one, New York. I went to Kearns again and he sighed, the guy could have sighed for the Olympics, and he snapped,

"What is it this time?"

I told him of the program and how I wanted New York.

He tut-tutted, there really is such a sound and it sounds ridiculous, unless you're a woman in her late seventies and even then. He said,

"That's for the best and the brightest."

I smiled and he said,

"Confident little bollix, aren't you?"

I gave him my best smile, I've practiced it, blends humility with the right amount of attitude. He said,

"I thought we were done with our little arrangements, you have, how shall we say, no further leverage, do you?"

I looked a bit bashful and said,

"I lied."

Now he was sitting up and I added,

"An underage girl you put the meat to, I have her sworn statement."

He couldn't believe it; he'd called in a lot of favors to get this to go away, but I'd pried a copy loose from the officer in charge, a guy who hated Kearns.

He debated on the prospect of telling me to go fuck meself but knew with the election coming up, this story would finish him. He said,

"It's going to take some time and I'm not sure I can swing it."

I said,

"I have every confidence in you."

He was right about one thing, it did take a while, and I walked those streets of Galway, the beads in the top pocket of my tunic. There was a woman, her car had stalled and she called me for assistance, I zoned but I do remember her beautiful neck, the rest is a blur. Those were still early times in my development of the beads and I took them with me when I was done.

Only later did it occur to me that to leave them would be like reverence.

Show me an honest cop
and I'll show you that pigs can fly.

—CONVICTED FELON TO A NEWSPAPER REPORTER

TWO

I HAD A GIRLFRIEND, IF YOU DIDN'T, YOU DIDN'T BLEND, and I knew how to do that. She didn't have that snow white long neck I adore and I think that's why I chose her, so she'd be in no danger.

Then I got a call from Kearns and he near shouted,

"It's done, you're with the NYPD for one year."

"Thank you so much, Mr. Kearns."

There was silence and he added,

"I hope they burn you fucking good."

And slammed the phone down.

I took the girl out for dinner and I think she thought I was

going to propose, instead I told her of my year assign-
ment to New York.

She had a mouth on her, went,

"Yah eejit, what do you want to go there for?"

Nearly said,

"To get the hell away from you."

Went with:

"For us, build us a better life."

Did she buy that?

Take a wild guess.

Said,

"Sure, we're the prosperous country now."

We danced around it for a bit but neither of us really
cared, and before I left, she said,

"I'd never have married a Guard anyway."

I could have said,

"And who was asking?"

She gave me a bottle of aftershave as a going-away present,
smelt like piss.

I could say she meant well.

She didn't.

I was listening to her, the green rosary in me pocket, zoning in and out . . . my eyes fixed on her neck, she was so blessed it was a mediocre one.

Few days before I left, I ran into this broken-down guy, had been on the force with my father. An alcoholic, he was some kind of half-arsed private investigator, he'd been dry for a few years then hit the bottle with ferocity and by Jaysus, the bottle hit back.

He looked like death warmed up. I lied, went,

"Mr. Taylor, you're looking well."

He gave me the look, said,

"You're full of shite."

It was in a pub, naturally.

One of the old ones, still unchanged, Garavan's, on Shop Street. Even had an Irish guy behind the pumps and believe me, the Irish are rarely to be found doing these jobs anymore.

Most likely, you'll find a woman from Nigeria or some guy from Lithuania behind the counter, and can they pour a pint?

Nope.

They just pour it straight into the glass, no time to sit, or get that creamy head settled.

They know about Bud, Coors, Miller.

Who doesn't?

Taylor still had the all-weather Guards coat and it was as
    battered as himself. I asked,

"Aren't you like, supposed to give that back?"

Not that I gave a feck but . . . chat, you know.

He sighed, said,

" 'Tis me only link to what once was . . ."

I thought that was pathetic, a frigging lousy coat, that's
    what he had to show for his life?

No wonder he drank.

I asked,

"Get you something?"

No hesitation.

"Jameson, pint of the black."

What the hell, I had the same.

We watched the guy build the pints with care and craft
    and he knew his trade, didn't bother us with nonsense
    like asking if we wanted ice in the whiskey.

The nonnationals, they don't ask, plunk ice in everything,
    especially their attitude.

We took our drinks to a corner table and he said,

"So you're going to the States?"

Galway, now a cosmopolitan city but still a village where
gossip was concerned. One of the reasons I wanted out.

Before I could answer, he said,

"And let me guess, you want to be on the NYPD?"

He might have been fucked in just about every way there
was but he still had that intuition.

I said I might consider it.

He raised his glass, a tremor in his hand, which we both
elected to ignore, said,

"Slainte."

Without hesitation, I threw back,

"*Leat fein.*" And you.

He shuddered as the whiskey hit his gut and followed it
fast with half his pint, get the sucker nailed down.

He wiped the cream from his lip, an old pro, and said,

"You want to carry a gun."

Jesus, he was good.

I said,

"That's not the reason I'd sign on."

He gave a bitter smile, the corners of his mouth turned down.

I saw a photo of Beckett in a mag once and fuck, more lines on his face than the ordnance map of the country.

Taylor's face would have given him a close run.

The lines were imbedded, like with a very sharp knife.

And the ones around his eyes, you just knew laughter certainly hadn't been responsible.

He said,

"Be sure you don't let the gun carry you."

Deep—or pure shite.

I said I'd bear it in mind.

And he said,

"You're the new Irish, you know that?"

I knew this wasn't flattery and asked,

"Yeah, what's that?"

He'd drained his pint, was signaling for another, said,

"Arrogance, confidence, and fuck-all ability."

Drink that.

As I got up to leave, he said,

"That darkness in you, get some help on it."

Fucking loser.

K-BAR: A SHORT STEEL POLE, HIGHLY EFFECTIVE IN SUBDUING CRIMINALS

THREE

KURT BROWSKI, BUILT LIKE A SHIT BRICKHOUSE AND JUST
as solid. A cop out of Manhattan South, he was having
a bad day.

Much like most days.

His heritage was East European but contained so many
strands, not even his parents knew for sure its exact
basis.

And cared less.

They wanted the American Dream.

Cash . . . and cash . . . and yeah, more of same.

They didn't get it.

Made them mean.

Very.

His mother was a cleaner and his father had been a construction worker but had settled into a life of booze, sure beat getting up at five o'clock in the morning.

His father beat his mother and they both beat Kurt.

Somehow he, if not survived them, got past them and finished high school, joined the cops.

He wanted to be where you gave payback.

That was how he saw the force, emphasis on *force*. He was certainly East European in his view of the boys in blue, they had the juice to lean on . . . whoever-the-fuck they wished.

And he did.

Hard.

His early weapon of choice was a K-bar.

Short, heavy and lethal and you could swing it real easy, plus, they rarely saw it coming.

They were watching your holstered gun and wallop, he slid the bar out of his sleeve and that's all she wrote.

His rep was built on it and over the years, he became known as Kebar.

Did he care?

Not so's you'd notice. He didn't do friends, so what the fuck did he care.

Sometimes though, he longed to go have a few brews with the guys, shoot the shit, chill. He adored country music, that sheer sentimentality was a large part of his nature and he kept it hidden. His fellow officers, they went to the bar, got a few put away, then played country and western till the early hours.

He loved Loretta Lynn, Ol' Hank of course, and then Gretchen Peters, Emmylou Harris, Iris DeMent, Lucinda Williams, they were his guilty pleasures. All that heartache, it was like they knew him.

His partners in the prowl car rarely lasted long, he took so many chances, they either got hurt real fast or transferred.

And now, you fucking believe it?

They were giving him some snot-nosed kid.

O'Brien, his commanding officer, a Mick, those guys, they still got the top jobs, had summoned him.

Anyone tell you the Micks were a thing of the past in the force . . . take a look at the roll call.

You think they were letting that lucrative line of not so equal opportunity slip away?

O'Brien didn't like Kebar, knew the guy was unhinged, but he sure got results and like O'Brien, he adhered to the old idea:

Justice was dispensed in alleys, not courtrooms.

He said to Kebar,

"Have a seat."

"I'll stand, sir."

Naturally.

O'Brien wondered if the guy ever eased up, said,

"Suit yourself."

He took a good look at Kebar.

The guy was all muscle, rage and bile.

Perfect cop for the times.

His face was a mess of broken nose, busted veins (he liked his vodka, straight), a scar over his left eye: he looked like a pit bull in uniform.

O'Brien said,

"Got you a new partner."

Kebar growled,

"Don't need no partner."

O'Brien smiled.

This is where it was good to be chief, flex that muscle, asked,

"I ask you what you needed? . . . Did you hear me do that? Yeah, it's not what you need, mister, it's what I tell you

you're getting. We have a reciprocal arrangement with the Irish goverment to take twenty of theirs and twenty of ours go over there."

Kebar had heard all this crap before . . . yada yada, he sighed, asked,

"Who am I getting?"

O'Brien was looking forward to this, opened a file, took out his glasses, all to annoy the shit out of Kebar, pretended to read:

"Matt O'Shea, did a year on the beat in Galway."

He paused, then added,

"Galway, that's in Ireland."

Kebar would have spit, reined it in a bit, sneered,

"A Mick, no disrespect, sir, but a greenhorn, gonna have to break his cherry for him?"

O'Brien was delighted, better than he'd hoped, he said,

"Actually, he seems a bright kid."

Kebar was enraged, rasped,

"In Ireland, they don't even carry freaking guns, they're like . . ."

He couldn't think of a suitable degrading term, settled for,

"Rent-a-cops."

O'Brien smiled again, he was having a fine morning, said,

"I'll expect you to treat him properly, that's all, dismissed."

Outside the office, Kebar spat, a passing cop was going to say something, saw who it was and kept on moving.

Kebar went down to the car pool, rage simmering in his belly, leaned against his car, got his flask out, drank deep. A young guy, in a sparkling new uniform, approached, put out his hand, asked,

"Officer Browski?"

Kebar stared at him, the new uniform was blinding, the gun belt neon in its newness, the buttons shining on his tunic.

He belched, grunted,

"Who's asking?"

The kid still had his hand out, his eyes full of gung ho bullshit, said,

"I'm your new partner, Matt O'Shea, they call me . . ."

Before he could go any further, Kebar said,

"Shut the fuck up, that's your first lesson, I want to know something, I'll ask you, can you follow that?"

"Yes, sir."

Sir.

Kebar thought it was going to be even worse than he'd imagined.

He asked,

"Can you drive?"

"Of course I . . ."

"Then get in the fucking car, get us out of here."

Kebar looked at his sheet, the assignments they'd pulled, and said,

"Head for Brooklyn, can you find that?"

Shea was going to tell him he now lived there but buttoned it, just nodded, thinking,

"Holy fook, I get a psycho on me first day."

They were passing an area of deserted lots, mud on the ground, no signs of habitation, and Kebar said,

"Pull up here."

Shea, nervous, before he could stop himself, went,

"Here?"

"Deaf as well?"

He pulled over.

Kebar got out, said,

"You hear of backup, get out of the fucking car."

Shea got tangled in his safety belt and harness, all the frigging equipment and it weighed a ton, plus, the uniform, Christ, how hot was it? And it itched.

Kebar said,

"Before the weekend, maybe?"

Shea, finally out, waited and Kebar said,

"Go, I'm behind you."

And for a wild moment, Shea wondered if the mad bastard was going to shoot him. The other cops had already told him of how Kebar's partners never lasted.

Before he could think beyond this, he got an almighty push in the back, sent him sprawling in the mud, covering his brand-new blues in crap and dirt.

He rolled round, tempted to go for his piece, Kebar was slugging from a flask, said,

"Now that's more like it, you don't look like such a freaking virgin. We go into the hood, they see that shiny new blue, we're meat."

And then he turned back to the car.

Shea watched his retreating bulk and hated him with a ferocity of pure intent.

As they drove off, Kebar was chuckling and Shea asked,

"You going to share the joke?"

Kebar looked at him, said,

"First day on the job, you're already a dirty cop."

They did a full day, settling domestics, leaning on dope dealers, cop stuff, some of it wildly exhilarating and most boring as hell.

And Shea, he never attempted to change his uniform or even brush the mud off it.

Kebar was impressed, he didn't let on but thought,

"Kid has cojones."

Even better, he didn't whine or complain, whatever nasty task Kebar set him, and he sure had some beauts, the kid just went at them, head down, his mouth set in a grim smile.

End of the shift, Kebar was tempted to say,

"You done good."

Went with:

"Early start tomorrow, don't be late."

The kid looked down at his feet, asked,

"You want to grab a cold one?"

And for a moment, Kebar nearly said yes, then reined it in, said,

"I don't drink with the help."

———

EVERYONE HAS THEIR ACHILLES' HEEL, THE ONE AREA that makes them vulnerable. From Bush to Bono, there is something they don't want known.

Be it pretzels or lack of height.

Kebar's was his sister, Lucia.

She had a serious mental handicap and now, in her thirties, she still had the face and mind of a five-year-old.

Their parents had been horrified and regarded her as a curse.

They had tried to beat it out of her, literally.

Now, she was in a very expensive home, where they treated her well, and she seemed, if not happy, at least less terrorized.

Out on Long Island, it cost a bundle to keep her there.

Kebar poured every nickel into her upkeep.

He was losing the battle.

The thought of her being put into one of the state institutions filled him with dread.

She'd been there already, courtesy of her parents, and suffered serious setbacks on every level.

Soon as Kebar could, he got her out of there, and into the new home.

The freight was killing him, he didn't go to ball games, or buy new clothes, every damn dime went to her.

It wasn't enough.

Enter the wiseguys.

A particular slice of sleaze named Morronni, feeling Ke-bar out and finally putting it to him:

"You need some serious wedge and we can give it to you."

How the fucks knew about Lucia, he didn't even ask, that was their gig, secrets.

He wanted to get his K-bar, ram it down the cocksucker's throat, but it was a week when he couldn't make the payments for Lucia so he asked,

"What've I gotta do?"

His heart in ribbons, he hated dirty cops with a vengeance and here he was, joining the ranks of the damned.

Morronni smiled, said,

"Hey, no big thing, you let us know when the cops are gonna make a bust, whose phones are tapped, small stuff, you know, nuttin to get in a sweat about."

Yeah.

Lure you in.

They did.

And progressed.

Bigger stuff.

The money was on a par.

He was able to guarantee six months ahead for Lucia.

The proprietor of the home, a sleek suit named Kemmel, said,

"Mr. Browski, we don't usually take large sums of cash. Checks, credit cards, they are the norm."

Kebar gave him his street look, the one that had serious skels looking away, said,

"Money is money, you telling me you can't do off the books, you want me to get the health department out here, give your place the once-over?"

No.

He took the money.

And in a sly tone asked,

"You need a receipt?"

Kebar wasn't used to being threatened, least not by pricks in suits, unless they were pimps, and certainly never twice.

Kemmel was sitting behind a large mahogany desk, smirk in place, not a single paper on the desk, a framed photo of his shiny wife and shinier kids facing out to the world, proclaiming,

"See, I'm a winner."

Kebar leaned across the desk, deliberately knocking the

frame aside, grabbed Kemmel by his tie, pulled him back across the desk, asked,

"You like fucking with me, that it?"

Kemmel, who'd never been manhandled in his life, was terrified, could smell garlic on the cop's breath, managed to croak,

"I think we might have hit a wrong note."

Kebar put his thumb up against Kemmel's right eye, said,

"One tiny push, and you'll see things in a whole different light."

Then he let him go, stood up, asked,

"You were saying?"

Kemmel, struggling for his dignity, adjusting his tie, said,

"No problem, Mr. B, I'll see to your . . . um . . . arrangement . . . personally."

Kebar edged the frame with his worn cowboy boots, his one indulgence, bought in the Village and custom-made, said,

"Real nice family, tell you what, I'll drive by, time to time, keep an eye on them, call it a *personal arrangement*."

The difference between a cop and a thug is one wears a uniform . . . sometimes.

—ED LYNSKEY, CONVICTED MURDERER

FOUR

NEXT DAY AT WORK, KEBAR WAS LEANING AGAINST THE
car, hoping the kid would be late.

He wasn't.

And the uniform, still mud encased.

Kebar asked,

"How'd the roster sergeant like your uniform?"

The kid said,

"He gave me a bollicking."

Kebar liked the term, had a nice ferocity about it, said,

"Tore you a new one, did he?"

The kid went,

"Tore what?"

Kebar laughed, he was going to have to teach him American as well as everything else, said,

"Asshole, we say, he tore me a new one, means you got reamed."

If the kid appreciated the lesson, he didn't show it.

Kebar was enjoying himself, it had been a long time since he enjoyed being buddied up.

He turned toward his door and he got an almighty push in the back, jammed him against the roof and then his arm was twisted up his back, the kid's arm round his windpipe, he heard,

"Let me teach you something, smartarse, the Guards, no matter what you think of them, they never forget . . . ever . . . and you ever push me in the fucking back again, you better be ready to back it up."

Then he let go.

Kebar was stunned, no one'd had the balls to come at him like that in a long time and he debated reaching for his bar, then began to laugh, said,

"You're a piece of work, you know that, let's roll."

The day's surprises weren't over yet. They answered a call to a domestic, and Kebar said,

"Don't get between the couple, nine times out of ten, you subdue the man, the freaking broad will gut you."

The kid said,

"Believe it or not, we have wife beaters in Ireland."

Kebar took a quick look at the kid, he was wearing a real serious expression, and Kebar asked,

"What you'd do, call the priest?"

Without changing his look the kid said,

"Often, 'tis the priest doing the beating."

Kebar liked that a lot, he was warming all the time to the punk, despite his best efforts.

They got to the scene, and Kebar led the way, his hand on his holster. The door of the apartment was open and a skinny white guy was whacking a woman like his life depended on it.

Kebar said,

"You want to stop doing that, sir?"

He didn't.

Said,

"Fuck off, pig, family business."

Kebar shrugged his sleeve, the bar sliding down, and he moved forward, missed seeing a side door open and a shotgun pointing out.

Two shots nearly deafened him and a body tumbled out, a guy moaning, he'd been hit in the shoulder and leg.

Kebar looked at the kid, his smoking gun still leveled. Kebar moved to the guy on the floor, kicked the shotgun away, said,

"Move and you're fucking dead."

The guy who'd been beating on his wife shouted,

"You shot my brother, you cocksucker."

Kebar took him out with the bar and then the woman started so she joined the bodies on the floor.

The kid still had the gun pointed.

Kebar said,

"You can put it down now."

The kid's eyes were clear and he nodded, said,

"Guess we better call it in."

They did.

Kebar moved to the kid, said,

"I owe you."

The kid gave him a look, said,

"Just backup, that's all, what is it you guys say? No biggie."

The brass arrived and reassured Shea it was *a good shoot* and even though Internal Affairs would be talking to him he had nothing to worry about, they actually clapped him on the back, said,

"You did real fine."

Outside, as they got into the prowl, Kebar said,

"Pretty fancy shooting."

The kid shrugged.

"I was aiming for what I figured was his head, need some practice I suppose."

They got out of there and back to the station house, Kebar broke his rule, asked,

"Can I buy you a brew, shit, lots of brews and what's that stuff you Micks like . . . Jameson?"

Shea stood for a moment, looking at the ground, then:

"No thanks, I'm the help . . . that's what you said . . . right?"

And he was gone.

Kebar felt let down, like he'd failed the kid.

What was for damn sure was, the kid hadn't failed him.

He got together the biggest and hardest men in the force and ordered them to go out and batter the living shite out of every ned.

—GLASGOW COP ON HIS BOSS, CHIEF PERCY SILLITOE

FIVE

WHEN I GOT TO NEW YORK, IT WAS EVERYTHING I'D HOPED for and more, loud, crazy, fierce, and I loved it.

I got lucky, an Irish guy who lived in Brooklyn was heading home and I got his place.

It was small but hey, I didn't have a whole lot of stuff.

A few shirts, jeans, one battered leather jacket, me Claddagh ring, heart turned out, and the beads, naturally.

You put them up against the window, the light gleamed, and I'd zone, mesmerized by the effect, seeing white slender beautiful necks, like the swans in the Claddagh basin.

The first time I took one of those animals, I nearly got caught but came out of the zone in time to get away.

When I was leaving Galway, my mother said,

"Son, I haven't been the best mother and I know you have some problems that need help but I got you this to show I do love you."

The Claddagh ring, one of the real old ones, it fit perfectly and I wore it all the time, heart turned out . . .

Meant I was on the hunt and I was.

A Miraculous Medal, never leave an Irish home without one, and two bottles of Jameson.

Oh yeah, hurley, got some funny looks from the Homeland Security guys but explained it was our national game and they let it slide.

The apartment had all I needed, hot plate, kettle, bed, and a shower.

Truth is, you couldn't swing a cat in it but I hate cats so . . .

Allowed meself a week to get orientated, that is, hit the bars, the Irish ones, get hooked up, get connected, and so, had me a beat-up Chevy in two days and then reported for duty.

The Mick ace helped, big time, and before I could say . . . muthafuckah, I was in.

I'm not going to be modest here, I'd done me training in Templemore and despite what the Yanks thought, it was tough, so the four weeks of orientation I had to do at the academy weren't really anything new, save for the pistol training.

You make some buddies, kiss arse big time, and keep your head down.

I kept me nose clean, in every sense, and did nowt for that month but focus on doing real good.

Only lost one rosary beads that whole time, well, lost is the wrong term, used it, more like.

I don't remember it too well save for it was the first time I left a beads behind, seemed to belong on her neck.

I continued to do real good in training.

And they like the Micks.

The powers that still be.

I used every suck-up going and in jig time I was assigned to a precinct.

I was dead freaking delighted with meself.

The commanding officer, a Mick, thank Christ, was happy to have as he called it:

"A real fucking Mick, off the boat," in his squad.

That morning, when I put on me uniform, and that sucker weighted, Jesus on a bike, did it ever, I put my cap on last and in the half mirror, left by the last tenant, I checked meself, had to crouch down which took from the whole effect but still, I saw the real deal looking back at me.

NYPD BLUE.

ME!

And my police issue on my hip, made me feel like a fucking player.

I was delighted with meself.

I'd done it, made me dream come true, I was the thin blue
line, I was *the man*, I was so delirious, I nearly had a
shot of Jameson.

Then, another Americanism I was to learn, things went
south.

My commander told me I was being paired with a real
pain in the ass and gave me a thumbnail sketch of
some guy called Kebar. I asked,

"Why?"

Thinking, "You're Irish, why are you not giving me some
slack?"

And he sighed, said,

"He's a real good cop, a massive pain in the butt, but if
you can hang in there, you'll learn stuff real fast, we
can't afford to have one of our visiting Guards get
lost."

I felt me temper rise, gritted,

"I'm a real fast learner."

He gave me a full-capped smile, said,

"See, that's the spirit, why I know you were the right guy
to partner up with him, but trust me, he'll bust your
balls nine ways to Sunday."

He sure did.

A surly bollix, he treated me like shite, in every way he could.

Even pushed me down in the dirt, no kidding, to get me good and dirty.

I bit down, took all his crap, and then I got him up against the car, told him who I was.

And Jesus, the same day, we were on a domestic, I got to use me gun, took out a guy with a shotgun, a rush like with the beads but too fast, no time to savor, *to linger.*

Saved the sour bastard's arse.

Pure dumb luck.

I was numb, never shot no one before and it was a trip, but after, I just went into the cold place.

They took my ice reaction as major cool, one man's trauma is another's rep.

I was in.

Saved a fellow cop, doesn't get any better.

And I blew it off, as if it was no big deal, and that impressed them even more.

Then Internal Affairs.

Fucking gobshites, we have our own version back home.

A sleazy level above rodents.

And the nearest thing to informers we've got in an official capacity. In Ireland, informers are beyond garbage, sold us out to the Brits every fecking time and just because they wore the same uniform, they were still the scum of the earth, selling out their own.

I was in a room with two of the creeps.

One big guy, said his name was McCarthy, like I was supposed to be grateful he had an Irish name, all I saw was a bum whose job was to screw his own kind.

He was all friendly but I wasn't buying it. He started,

"Matt, you mind if I call you Matt?"

I gave him my stonewall look and he said,

"Matt it is, now, we have what certainly seems to be a good shooting, but how about you walk us through it, cover all the bases."

The other guy, a black dude, was leaning against the wall, chewing on a matchstick, his eyes fixed on me, least that's what I first thought, then realized he was fixated on me ring. I said,

"We answered a domestic call, we got there, my partner tried to separate a husband who was walloping his missus and then I saw a shotgun come out a door."

McCarthy put up his hand to stop me, asked,

"And did you caution him, tell him to drop his weapon, identify yourself as a police officer?"

I glanced at the black guy and was he smiling? I asked,

"You ever hear a shotgun being primed?"

He stared at me, irritation on his face, asked,

"What's your point?"

I made a click with my tongue, said,

"That's the sound and it tells you, you have maybe two seconds to identify yourself or . . . save your partner, what would you do or don't you get out from behind a desk?"

The black guy chuckled and McCarthy was riled, snapped,

"Hey pal, you're a goddamn rookie, don't get mouthy with me, you got that?"

I let that hover for a bit, then said,

"A rookie who saved his partner's life."

He changed tactics, became Mr. Cordiality, asked,

"How do you find your partner, busting your balls is he?"

Now I got to smile, said,

"I thought that was your job."

He let it go, continued,

"How do you feel about cops on the take?"

I didn't hesitate, said,

"Much the same way I feel about informers, sorry . . . Internal Affairs."

He jumped up, leaned right in my face, and if he expected me to flinch, he was wrong.

In Templemore, the first month of Guards enlistment, you have training officers from the Midlands, big country fuckers who play hurling because they love the brutality, they are thick bastards and as tough as granite, and they spend that first month shouting, spittle included, into your face.

You get through that, and learn early . . . never . . . ever, wipe the spit off, you can face any fucker roaring into your mouth. He shouted,

"Listen up, Paddy, you're going to be seeing a lot more of me, and you don't know it yet but IA might be a bigger part of your life than you ever imagined, that is, if you intend staying on the force."

He pulled back, well pleased with his threat. I asked,

"Can I ask a question?"

"Knock yourself out, I'm a Mick too, remember?"

"What happened to you calling me Matt?"

He spat on the floor, said,

"Get out of my fucking office."

I was at the door and I said,

"McCarthy, despite your name, I think you got the wrong country in your heritage."

He was curious, thinking maybe I was making amends, he asked,

"Yeah, where should I be from?"

I let a beat go, then said,

"Nazi Germany."

I swear, the black guy winked.

That black guy, whose name was Rodriguez, there was something about him, a familiarity, as if I'd known him before, and it took me a while to figure it out, I was staring in the mirror, a habit I'd become more and more addicted to.

Not out of vanity but there was a little of that, I'm a good-looking guy, so some of that but primarily, to try and see if the two sides of my nature showed, they hadn't . . . yet.

After Internal Affairs, when I stared in the mirror, I saw Rodriguez, that was it, he had that same dark shadow on his soul.

An echo in the darkness.

I was pretty pleased with meself but as usual, my frigging mouth had made me a bad enemy.

If the blue menaces are ever going to catch me, they had better get off their fat butts and do something.

—THE ZODIAC, LETTER TO THE *LOS ANGELES TIMES,* 1971

SIX

RIDING WITH KEBAR AFTER, THE WHOLE DYNAMIC HAD
changed, he no longer gave me grief and Jesus, asked
my opinion on stuff, like if we were going into a crack
house, he'd go,

"How d'you want to play this . . . partner?"

Even he seemed stunned by his behavior, as if he'd lost his
way and was floundering.

Fuck, I let him flounder.

The bollix had gone out of his way to make me life hell,
and now he didn't know his arse from his elbow, he
even forgot one time to slide the bar up his sleeve till I
reminded him.

Our luck stayed golden and we brought down a major

dope dealer by pure chance, it was a collar that made the front pages of the *Daily News*.

Kebar said,

"This rate, kid, you'll make detective in no time."

And thing is, I felt blessed, bulletproof, no matter what I touched, it panned out. I'm Irish, I should have known better, things go that well, God is seriously screwing with you, seeing just how much you think it is your sheer talent before He fucks you good.

I was learning the lingo, my American coming in daily, still had me brogue of course and it amused the other cops to hear me cuss American with an Irish accent but at least I was getting there.

I noticed they had picked up a few of mine too, even Kebar had started calling creeps "bollix" and I once heard him say . . .

"Things were fierce."

Best of all was when we pulled in a vicious hooker who had been slashing johns and he said, as she tried to bite him,

"Fuck on a bike."

Had him.

A month flew by in a haze, and knocking off work, Kebar asked,

"There's a bar in Brooklyn, got some great beer, I'd, um . . .

you know, appreciate it if you let me . . . buy you a few brews."

I figured he'd done enough penance, said,

"Sounds good."

His whole face lit up and to see him smile, it was a whole other guy, like he was ten years old.

We arranged to meet at eight o'clock and as I headed for the locker room, he went,

"Shea?"

First time he used me name, and I turned. He said,

" 'Preciate it."

I said,

"Whatever."

I was going to cut him some slack but not get stupid either.

Little did I know.

I got back to my place, I showered, broke out a cold one and rolled a little weed, nothing major, just chill on out, fingered the green rosary, the need was mounting.

This was always the roughest time, as the darkness mounted and demanded its due, the other side of me, *the good cop*, wanted to be a regular guy and, here's the joke, to meet a woman who would so consume me that I wouldn't need the long slender necks of others. The zoning was becoming more powerful and the durations longer, how much of any decency was left was eroding rapidly.

I had the TV on, listened to the news, a hundred Americans killed in Iraq in one month.

Jesus.

I turned it off, sank back in a chair, lit up the spliff, took a long draw of the Miller, hit the radio, a station playing old hits.

"Tainted Love" by Soft Cell, I sang along with the chorus, the weed chilling me way out.

My uniform was hanging on the back of the door, and I gazed at it, still in amazement it was actually mine.

I said,

"Fuck, you son of a gun, you really did it."

I had bigger plans, no way was I going home after a year, I fully intended being a hero cop and then no way could they send me home, that precinct, it would be mine, I'd already started gleaning information, like that O'Brien liked young girls, I'd gather me ammunition and then when my plans were full crystallized, I'd hit like that cobra.

Back home, the lads would be getting ready to go out for a few pints.

For few, read fifteen.

Jaysus, if they could see me now.

Was this the American Dream?

Fecking would be if I made detective, and the way I was cruising, what could stop me?

Dumb fuck I am, I'm Irish, superstition is our birthright but did I bless meself, touch wood, do any ritual stuff?

Nope.

Bad fuck to it now, would it have changed anything?

Wouldn't have hurt.

But no, I opened another brew, and here were U2 with *still haven't found what I'm looking for.*

I had, hadn't I?

Damn straight, my accent coming in.

I figured I should eat something and the weed had given me the munchies so I called out for some pizza.

The guy arrived in like jig time and I spotted him a five, he looked at me, said,

"Cop, right?"

I was delighted, asked,

"How'd you know?"

He gave that New Yorker look, said,

"Cop lives in the building, everyone hides their stash."

Then he wrinkled his nose, smelling the weed, said,

"Evidence, huh?"

I put my fingers to my lips, made the shssssh noise.

He was cool, down with it, said,

"You ever need some decent blow, you gimme a call, my name is Jimmy."

I asked,

"Jimmy, how come you think I won't bust your arse?"

"Ass, you're in America now, and you're Irish, the Irish don't give a fuck, see yah."

And he was gone, whistling what might well have been "Galway Bay" but that was probably the weed.

The pizza was good and I felt wired, good to go, good to . . . boogie.

I didn't have a whole lot of clothes so wore a white T . . . whitish, and black 501s, a pair of knock-off Nikes and me one sports jacket.

Whatever else it said, it sure as shite said, *he's not on the take.*

A line that would come back to haunt me.

In my mind, I saw the green rosary . . . gleaming.

KEBAR WAS IN THE LOCKER ROOM, FEELING PLEASED THE kid had agreed to have a brew.

He asked himself why it was so important.

He'd never wanted buddy stuff before.

But then, nobody had ever saved his life either.

If the kid hadn't stepped up to the plate, Kebar would be pushing up dirt, and he shuddered:

What would Lucia do if he was gone?

Back to the state garbage bins.

Yeah, he owed and not just for himself, Lucia too, so the least he could do was buy the kid some cold ones, maybe let him in on stuff that would take years to learn.

Clean the slate.

He'd never owed before and it was confusing him.

Plus, fuckit, he liked the kid, who'd have ever seen that coming?

Kebar hadn't liked anyone in . . . jeez . . . when . . . ever?

The other cops, they gave Kebar a wide berth, you bid him the time of day, he growled right back at you.

But the older guys, they didn't much like him, what was

there to like, he was a surly mean bastard, but they sure as shit respected him, he was your real beat cop, a stand-up guy, and he believed in the old ways.

A sergeant, a Polack named Swierzcynski, approached Kebar, asked,

"Got a moment, K?"

Kebar, who should have been a sergeant long ago 'cept for his attitude, snapped,

"Make it quick."

The sergeant sighed, hard to help this schmuck but he tried, said,

"You need to watch your back."

Kebar stopped, turned, asked,

"What's that mean?"

The sergeant checked they couldn't be heard, said,

"IA is sniffing around you."

Kebar shrugged it off, said,

"Fuck 'em, they got nothing on me."

The sergeant, knowing he was going way out there, said,

"You got a sister?"

Kebar was stunned, he'd kept her real hidden, asked,

"How do you know?"

The sergeant gave a rueful smile, said,

"I hear stuff and the word is, she's in a real fancy home . . ."

Pause.

"A very expensive one."

Kebar was thinking,

"Fuck fuck fuck."

But he said nothing and the sergeant added,

"Word is they're using the kid to bring you down."

Kebar couldn't help it, splurted,

"That kid saved my ass."

The sergeant shook his head, said,

"That's why he's perfect to take you down, you trust him."

Kebar gave a grudging thanks and the sergeant said,

"Not too many good ones left."

Kebar got out of there quick, thinking,

"Damn kid, he wouldn't turn, would he?"

He had to hustle to get to see Lucia before he met with the kid. The drive out to Long Island was the usual fucking nightmare, and he got there running way late so he'd have to cut his time with his sister short.

Thus preoccupied, he never clocked the tail on his ass.

And if he had, he'd have been sure it was Internal Affairs.

He'd have been wrong.

As he went in, the Chevy pulled in a few spaces behind his car. The driver sighed,

"How long will the prick be, liked, visiting?"

Morronni, on his cell phone in the backseat, said,

"I'm told he's meeting the Irish guy . . ."

He checked his gold Rolex, he knew the time to the second but he liked to flash the bling, said,

"At eight, so he's gonna have to cut the time with the spastic short."

The driver, not really giving a fuck, asked,

"That what she is, huh?"

Morronni said,

"The fuck do I know, some kind of retard is all, what's it matter?"

It didn't.

Kebar hated to cut her time, but maybe she wouldn't notice, he'd brought her Hershey's Kisses.

Her ritual was always the same, she'd count them out.

"One for Daddy, one for Mamma, one for Konny," her childhood name for him, "and one for little old me."

Fuck, to see your beautiful thirty-five-year-old sister do that, when she should be married with two kids and a halfway decent husband, it shriveled his heart.

She had her own room, the room of a five-year-old girl, childish pictures on the wall, a comforter on the bed with the Care Bears, and a galaxy of dolls on the shelf with nursery rhyme books alongside.

Her hair was in ringlets, her huge brown eyes, not a trace of guile in them, and the button nose. Barney was on the TV . . . and she was singing along to the theme song.

Kebar hated that fucking purple dinosaur with all his soul.

He said,

"How yah doing, hon?"

She jumped up, threw herself into his arms, showering his face with kisses, he wanted to shoot some fucker, now.

He gave her the bag of goodies and she shrieked in delight, sat on the bed and said,

"Come sit beside me, Konny, we'll count out the Kisses."

Every time, it wounded him anew.

She asked,

"How is Daddy?'

The piece of no-good trash who'd beaten her senseless so many times, he wanted to go,

"Dead, thank fuck."

Said,

"He's working real hard, gonna get you that playhouse soon."

The fuck worked like one week his whole whining life.

"And Mammy?"

Tell the truth?

"Loaded before noon, progressed to margaritas now and which with any luck will kill the bitch soon."

Sure, tell that.

He said,

"She's knitting you a scarf for when the winter comes and you can come home."

Same goddamn lie he'd been telling for years.

Lucia asked, a slight frown between her innocent eyes,

"They sure love us, don't they, Konny?"

"You betcha."

And here came the same question, every visit, every
time,

"Tell me how much?"

This might be always the hardest lie of all, he stretched his
arms as wide as he could, said,

"To the moon and all the way back again."

The words nigh choking him.

It did the trick though. She gave that radiant smile that
age would not wither, nor time erase.

She sang along with the end credits of Barney and then
yawned, said,

"It's time for my nap, will you tuck me in?"

He did and kissed her gently on the forehead.

She was asleep before he reached the door.

He didn't look back, that one step he could never take, seeing her sleeping, her face like every wonderful thing
that never happened.

In the corridor, a nurse asked,

"Leaving so soon?"

He was going to go,

"The fuck does that mean?"

But said,

"She's sleeping."

And got the hell out of there, checked his watch, he might just make the appointed time.

We're exactly like you cops. You have a profession—we have a profession. Only difference is, you're on the right side of the law, we're on the wrong.

—JOHN DILLINGER

SEVEN

TRAFFIC WAS LIGHT, AND HE YET AGAIN FAILED TO SEE
the Chevy behind. He was pulling into a space near
the bar as he saw the kid saunter along.

Watched him for a moment, then opened his glove com-
partment, took out his Glock, put it in the waistband
of his pants, closed his eyes for a moment, then got
out, shouted,

"Yo, Shea, wait up . . . buddy."

If the kid was pleased to see him, he was hiding it well, just
nodded, noncommittal.

They entered the bar without another word.

The place had a pool table, a long wooden bar, and lots of
tables at the back. They moved up to the counter.

A tall girl, dark hair, eyes, an almost pretty face, spoiled by a too large nose with a good body, and a name tag . . . Nora.

Shea thought,

"Jaysus, not a bloody Mick, please?"

And tried not to stare at her neck, that white white flesh, and soft . . . Jesus.

The last shite he wanted to hear was reminiscences about the old country, the usual blarneyed lies.

She smiled, a good one. Asked,

"Get you gentlemen?"

Kebar said,

"Maker's Mark, Bud back."

And she looked to Shea.

He was so relieved to hear her New York accent, he went,

"Got any Jameson?"

She smiled, like . . . gee, what a surprise, said,

"Sure."

"Okay, with a Coors."

She gave him an odd look and he thought,

"What? . . . Like I'd frigging drink Guinness outside Ireland, yeah, dream on, babe."

She asked,

"You running a tab?'

Kebar nodded. They took their drinks to a rear table, Kebar raised his shot glass, said,

"Here's to partners."

Shea clinked the Jay against it, said,

"Why not."

They took a swish of their beers, then sat back.

Neither one had a damn word to say.

Shea tried not to think about her neck.

KEBAR HEADED TO THE BAR TO GET REFILLS AND THUS missed Morronni walking in.

Morronni, delighted with his timing, went straight up to Shea, sat down, put out his hand, sliding an envelope on the table, bills protruding, said,

"Carmelo Morronni."

Shea, taken aback, took his hand, and Morronni said,

"Smile, you're on *Candid Camera*."

A flash went off, Morronni's man smiled, put the camera away, and Morronni put the envelope in his pocket.

Shea growled,

"The fuck is that about?"

Morronni said,

"Call it insurance."

Kebar came back, his face a mask of fury at seeing Morronni sitting there. Shea said,

"This guy took me photo, with a wad of money on the table and me shaking hands with him."

Kebar put the drinks down, carefully, looked to Morronni's man, said,

"Give me the camera."

The guy smiled, pulled his jacket back to show the Magnum in his belt, said,

"Come and take it, asswipe."

Morronni cut in, said,

"Whoa, compadres, chill out, Gino, go get us some drinks, bourbon rocks, how about you guys, you good?"

Kebar was still standing, considering taking the camera. Morronni said,

"Come on, K, have a seat and let's fill your young buddy in on the current state of play."

Kebar sat and Shea asked,

"What the fuck is going on, who are these guys?"

Morronni smiled, said,

"We're your business associates, but K can explain better,
   right, bro? Tell him how you work for us and as Jackie
   Gleason used to say . . . *how sweet it is.*"

Kebar was lost, couldn't look at the kid, he gulped the
   bourbon in one swallow. Shea looked from one man to
   the other, realization dawning, said,

"You're on the take . . . you . . . Jesus Christ, and you
   brought me here, to what . . . suck me in . . ."

His rage was blinding him, as he saw the net they'd thrown,
   he looked at Kebar, said,

"Fuck you."

And stood up. Morronni said,

"Whoa, kid, calm down, no need to get riled up, and we
   do have your picture, you don't want that on your
   boss's desk tomorrow, do you?"

Shea leaned over, right in Morronni's face, said,

"Screw you, bollix."

Then to Kebar,

"Get that fucking picture back."

And walked out.

Kebar wanted to go after him and say what?

He stared at Morronni, asked,

"Why'd you have to involve the kid?"

Morronni took a delicate sip of his drink and then, using a dazzling white handkerchief, dabbed at his mouth, said,

"Keep you focused."

Kebar was trying to get his mind in gear, said,

"You have me, I'm doing all you ask, give me the photo and we can forget this ever happened."

Morronni stood up, threw a hundred on the table, said,

"Drinks on me, and Gino, he doesn't like you, K, I'd advise against trying to force him to do anything he's not kosher with, that Magnum of his? I'd say it balances out the bar you carry. We'll be in touch."

And they were gone.

Kebar sat, the mess of glasses on the table reflecting the total chaos of his mind.

Nora came over, asked,

"They upped and left you?"

He nodded and she pushed,

"The young guy, he married?"

Kebar looked at her, said,

"The fuck would I know."

She picked up the hundred, said,

"I'll get your change."

Kebar was up, said,

"Keep it."

She watched him slump out, the weight of the world on his shoulders. The young guy, though, he was kinda cute, first thing after her shift was done, she'd ring Joe, her brother, tell him that just maybe . . . there might be a guy on the horizon.

KEBAR WAS WAITING AT THE CAR FOR THE KID, THE NEXT morning, he didn't know if the kid would even show.

He did.

Looking like ferocity.

Kebar tried,

"We need to talk about that whole fiasco last night."

Shea stared at him contempt written on his face, said,

"I've asked for a meeting with O'Brien, I'm going to ask for reassignment."

Kebar was afraid of this, said,

"C'mon, don't do that, let me at least explain."

Shea let that hover for a moment then said,

"You're a bagman, isn't that the term, you sell cops for money, what's to explain."

Kebar said,

"Get in the car, I want to show you something."

For a moment, it seemed like the kid wouldn't but Kebar went,

"Please."

He did.

Drove out to Long Island, no talk the whole trip, each man buried in his own shell. They got to the nursing home and Shea asked,

"What the fuck is this?"

Kebar got out, said,

"Come on."

Led him to Lucia's room, she was watching the Teletub-bies. Kebar said,

"Hon, this is my partner, his name is Shea, will you mind him for a moment?"

Before Shea could object, Kebar was gone and he was left alone with this lovely-looking woman who had the eyes of a child.

She gave him a radiant smile, asked,

"Would you like a kiss?"

Then laughed, said,

"A chocolate one."

Shea didn't know what to do so he took the Hershey's Kiss and she watched him, said,

"Aren't they dreamy?"

He nodded, all his speech seemed to have dried up.

He was fixated on her neck, the whitest, most beautiful he'd ever seen.

Then he managed,

"What's your name?"

She gave him that child's look of disbelief, like, was he so dense?

Said,

"I'm Lucia, Konny's sister."

Konny?

She took out a notebook, asked,

"Want to play tic-tac-toe?"

He didn't.

But did.

Trying to get a handle on what the deal was.

Kebar was looking for a coffee machine, and Kemmel, the proprietor of the home, came along the corridor, wearing a very expensive suit. Kebar knew expensive gear, as he could never afford it. This was one of those suits, you could sleep in it and it would still be up before you, looking wonderful. He had a bright red tie with some goddamned crest on it. He asked,

"Ah, Mr. B, I wonder if I might have a word?"

"Make it a quick one."

Kemmel indicated his office and Kebar followed him in, noticed a percolator on the shelf, hot coffee simmering, didn't ask, went and poured himself a mug. Kemmel, in his best therapeutic tone, asked,

"Need a doughnut, bagel, to go with that?"

Kebar said,

"I need anything, you'll know, what's eating you this time?"

Kemmel sat on the side of his desk, keeping it informal, carefully adjusted the crease in his pants, and Kebar, to his fascination, noticed the prick's socks were held up by straps.

Jesus.

Kemmel cleared his throat. Kebar usually reached for his piece when a guy did that, meant he was about to make a play.

Kemmel said,

"We try to keep our patients as content as we can and not to unduly alarm them if that's possible."

Kebar was familiar with shit sandwiches, first the savory then the crap, he waited.

Kemmel continued, his voice faltering a little,

"So, you visiting, and don't get me wrong, we love to see how often you do, but um . . . would it be possible for you to . . . ahem, leave the uniform at home . . . gun belts . . . they, uh, upset the status quo."

Kebar stood up, said,

"No."

Walked out.

He could hear Lucia laughing as he approached the room, knocked and went in. Shea was actually smiling and Lucia was clapping her hands in delight.

Kebar asked,

"How you guys getting along?"

Lucia crooned,

"He's lovely and such a good sport."

Kebar gave her a hug, said,

"We got to roll, hon, but I'll be back later."

She smiled, asked,

"And will you bring Shea?"

Kebar looked at him. Shea said,

"I'd be honored to come."

She threw her arms round him, said,

"I'm going to marry you when I grow up."

Shea had to bite down not to put his hands on her neck.

A vulnerable cop is a dead cop.

—STREET DEALER IN THE PROJECTS

EIGHT

THEY DIDN'T SPEAK TILL THEY GOT TO THE CAR, SHEA looked up at the building, asked,

"How long has she been here?"

Kebar stopped, then,

"Too long."

They'd been cruising for about ten minutes when Kebar said,

"Now you know."

Shea didn't answer.

They got through their shift, a relatively quiet day,

rounding up hookers, busting the balls of some street dealers, penny ante stuff.

The end of the shift, Kebar asked,

"What are you thinking?"

Shea didn't look at him, said,

"I'm real sorry about your sister, but it doesn't change the facts."

"The facts?"

"You're a cop on the take, you're no longer fit to wear the uniform, my uniform was dirty, but you, your whole existence is rotten."

And he was gone.

KEBAR TOOK SOME SICK DAYS SO I WAS ASSIGNED TO A desk till he returned. My mind was a whirlwind of conflicting emotions. Sure, I thought about his sister, I'd never seen a neck so fucking virgin, so fucking pure, and here's an odd thing, I know fuck all about James Joyce, like most Irish people. Not that we'd ever admit it, we claim him as our great writer, but read him?

Nope.

My mother still clung to the notion that he wrote *dirty books.*

But I do know the intense pain of his life was his beloved daughter being confined to a mental hospital.

Her name:

Lucia.

Riddle me that.

And more, meeting the bar person, Nora, Joyce's wife was
  Nora.

What did it all mean?

Fucked if I knew.

A week behind a desk, and I was stir-crazy.

I loved the streets and maybe Kebar would resign and I
  could get a new partner, new start.

That Nora was occupying me thoughts a lot and okay . . .
  I was zoning a bit, more so than I'd ever before and
  the beads . . . gleaming . . . waiting . . . and no longer
  asking . . . demanding.

So I headed back there one evening and she smiled, said,

"Jameson, Coors back."

I said,

"Can I run a tab?'

She was smiling broadly and I went,

"What?"

"I love your accent."

I heard, yeah, the word . . . *love.*

Lame . . . right.

I downed the Jameson and she asked,

"Where's your partner?"

I said,

"He'd got some sick time coming."

Her face showing concern, she asked,

"Is he sick?"

I thought, "He sure is going to be."

I said,

"Naw, just skiving off."

She looked at her watch, said,

"It's my break, you want to join me at the staff table while
    I grab a sandwich?"

Sure.

A sandwich in Ireland is dead bread, with a mangy slice of
    lettuce and some cut of synthetic meat, but here, shite,
    a triple decker of goodies and huge plates of chips . . .
    sorry, fries.

She ate like a navvy, with gusto and not caring about mayo
    leaking down her chin, Jesus, I loved that.

I kept me eyes off her neck, the time would come.

She indicated her plate, said,

"Dig in."

Not when I'm drinking, get a nice buzz building and screw
    it up with food, no way.

I asked,

"Nora . . . you're not Jewish, I'd say?"

That marvelous laugh again and she said,

"Third-generation Mick."

And before I could respond, she said,

"I grew up in a house with Irish music playing . . . all the
    freaking day, and on the walls, harps, bodhrans, pic-
    tures of the pope, John F. Kennedy, and of course a
    massive portrait of the Sacred Heart."

I laughed, could be any home in old Galway.

She said,

"Tell you the truth, I'm sick of the whole patriotic gig."

I couldn't resist, said,

"Ah, you turncoat."

She stared at me, asked,

"So, you're a cop, you like that?"

I told the truth.

"I love it."

The bar was filling up and she said,

"Gotta go earn the bucks, hey, you want to take me out on Friday night?"

I did.

I left the bar, floating on air, the Jameson had something to do with it but Jesus, I liked how near she was to answering the call of the beads, but riding point was the other side of me, could she be the one who would so occupy me that the beads would be . . . just a beads, no light, no shimmer, no . . . translucence?

Right there and then, I thought nothing could burst me balloon of well-being.

I was wrong.

Got back to me apartment, the door off the hinges, had been kicked in.

I pulled out my police issue, had taken to carrying it since meeting the wiseguys.

Entered slowly, the place was destroyed, my few possessions torn and scattered on the floor, a huge turd in the middle of the room and urine all over the place.

The worst, my uniform, hanging on the door, they'd taken a knife to it, shredded it. The gun in my hand was drenched in sweat and I had to ease the trigger back, slowly.

Then I saw the note on the table.

It was in red marker, read:

TIS A PITY.

I muttered,

"Bollix can't spell."

They'd missed the beads, stupid fucks, with all that came
   after, that would have proved their case . . . dumb bastards.

The wiseguys, taking the war to me and letting me know
   I was . . . touchable.

I said aloud,

"Fuck you, Kebar, look at the shite you've got me in."

And then I giggled, thinking of all the plans I'd made and
   if only they'd found the beads, I yelled aloud,

"Yah stupid fucks, if only you had any idea."

I cleaned up as best as I could and finally headed for the
   camp bed, pulled back the blanket and there was the
   photo, me shaking hands with Morronni, the envelope
   of bills spilling out.

What they call a damning indictment.

Man, they thought they were setting me up . . . if only they
   had one iota of how they were actually helping me.

Odd thing, I dreamt of that swan in Galway, the way it

struggled, and the sounds it made and how I'd tried to hush it, telling it I loved it.

ONE VITAL LESSON YOU LEARN AS A GUARD IS . . . THEY threaten you, you either run like a bastard, or . . . you get right back in their face.

Immediately.

Brutally.

Biblically.

And I wanted to.

Shite on my floor, me beloved uniform in tatters.

Fuck that.

You go after the messenger first, the fuckhead who left the calling card, like that song . . . *First, we take Manhattan.*

Then you let that simmer and in jig time, you take after the head honcho.

Gino, I remember Morronni calling his rent-a-thug that.

And how hard would it be to find that piece of lowlife?

You're in the NYPD . . . you have access, and if not to all areas, certainly where the bottom feeders dwell.

At the station I got on the computer, and he had a rap sheet as long as an Irish story, all intimidation gigs.

This guy liked to terrorize people.

Okay.

He played pool in a dive in the Village three nights a
week.

I fingered the green rosary, thinking . . . buddy, this beads
is gonna put you away . . . for ever.

Time to introduce him to our national sport.

Hurling.

A blend of hockey and homicide.

I put the hurley in a carryall, me police issue in the waistband of me jeans, and I was good to go.

I'd let meself get into the zone.

You replay the guy trashing your home, violating your
gear, and imagine him doing it with a smirk.

You've entered the zone.

I'd scored some stuff from Jimmy the pizza guy and
crunched a speed tab, washed it down with a shot of
Jay, and headed out.

The dive was certainly that.

In the middle of a fairly prosperous part of the Village, it
stood out like a Brit at an Irish wedding, defiant and
sneering.

I went in, lots of bikers, lots of attitude, the bar guy, big and I bet with a baseball bat under the counter, snarled,

"Get you?"

"Coors."

Eyeballing me but I let that slide, he wasn't my interest.

I put a couple of bucks on the counter, moved off to the side.

The pool table was hopping, lots of action, money laid on the side, and there he was.

Gino.

Living it up.

You want to get a guy's attention, take his knees out first with a hurley.

—IRISH GUARD ON POLICING METHODS

NINE

DRESSED IN WHAT WE CALL A WAISTCOAT AND FOR INEX-
plicable reasons the Yanks call a vest. A very shiny
number and tight trousers, I could see the piece against
his backbone, the butt of it outlined against his vest
when he bent to take a shot.

Let them know he was carrying.

His face was covered in sweat and he was downing shoot-
ers like a good un.

He'd need to piss . . . right.

He did.

Shouting to his opponent,

"Gotta take a goddamn leak, be right back to hand you
your ass."

And he pushed his way to the restroom.

I followed.

He was in one of the stalls and I locked the door, got out the hurley, he was grunting like a pig and finally sighed, came out, saw me, went,

"The fuck . . ."

Took his legs out with the hurley.

Swoosh.

I love that sound, clean, efficient, and highly effective.

He was on his knees in the piss on the floor, moaning, and I gave him another wallop to the side of the head, not to knock him out but to focus him.

Then I stood over him, the hurley resting lightly on my shoulder.

He looked up, muttered,

"You're fucking dead, pal."

Wallop.

Left shoulder, spread it around.

I said,

"This is the lesson of the ash, what our hurleys are made from, and the lesson teaches next time, it's your head only that gets the walloping."

I asked,

"Where's the photo?"

He dredged up some phlegm, spat it at me feet, I said,

"That is a really disgusting habit."

Gave him a tap on the nose, broke it, said,

"Have some fucking finesse."

I reached down, shoved him against the wall, got his wallet out and said,

"Pay for the damage to my place."

Must have been four, five hundred bucks, I took it all, flicked the wallet in the toilet, said,

"Next time you come after me, bring more than a note."

And put his lights out.

Back in the bar, I drained the Coors and the bar guy asked,

"Another?"

I shook me head, said,

"Your restroom, it's got shite all over the floor."

Got out of there fast.

I hailed a cab, went uptown and found a flash-looking bar, went in, ordered a double Jay, and when it came, I had to wait a full five minutes for me hands to stop shaking before I could lift it.

It had been a while since I played hurling.

But you never quite lose the talent, and to hear that whoosh of the bat, it was like the darkest music.

KEBAR HAD BEEN ON A SIX-DAY BENDER, YOUR NO-HOLDS- barred, out-and-out blitz. Two-fisted drinking, with serious intent. You name it, he sank it, Dewar's, Stoli, tequila . . . hello . . . tequila? . . . Wild Turkey, Early Times and early it wasn't, gallons of brews, from Shiner to Sam Adams, an equal opportunity imbiber.

Food, right . . . if you count Kentucky Fried Chicken, Burger King Whoppers, pizza, Chinese, and whatever clogs your arteries, gives you the cholesterol jibbies, he had it.

And course, you have a hard-on for the world, and you drink like that, trouble is gonna come down the pike with a vengeance and that's what he wanted.

To crack skulls, lash out, annihilate every fucker who even glanced at him.

And they did.

Paid the price.

Kebar was a big Springsteen fan, "The Price You Pay" unreeling in his head like a dodgy old 45.

And get this, when you have the out-on-the-precipice dementia, there's going to be oddities thrown into the maelstrom.

Emily Dickinson, not the first name you'd have put in this cauldron but logic hadn't a whole lot of validity in this gig.

And . . . in German.

He had no idea how that happened but he had a battered copy of her *Guten Morgen, Mitternacht.*

And add to the mystery, he could quote from it, where'd that come from?

Fuck knows.

As he brought the bar down on some skel's head, he incanted:

"Tod macht die Saiten krumm—

Nicht meine Schuld."

". . . Death twists the strings—

'Twasn't my fault."

And his mantra:

"Ein fremder Stamm, allein—"

. . . Wrecked, solitary, here—

He fucking loved that.

When he would finally stagger back to his crap one-room

apartment in Queens, he'd throw up the food he'd bought, pour a lethal shot of Stoli, thinking,

"Mellow on down."

He'd drag his battered suitcase from under the bed, flip it open, and his stone face would nearly smile.

His pride and joy.

Weapons.

Glock, Beretta, snub-nosed .22, and the beauty, the Smith & Wesson .44 Magnum.

Serious firepower.

He loved that elephant, the wood grip, the sheer weight in your hand, you hit a freak with that, he wasn't never getting up again.

He'd put Bruce on the turntable, "Thunder Road," "State Trooper," "Stolen Car," and he was wired.

The Magnum in his right hand, the thought of eating the barrel occurring more and more.

One squeeze, no more crap.

Late on a Friday, *Deadwood* on the box, he had the piece to his mouth when his door received a bang.

Holding the weapon loosely by his side, he opened it.

Morronni, a box of pizza and a bottle of merlot, said,

"Beware of goons bearing gifts, right?"

He glanced down at the Magnum, asked,

"You expecting company or just riled up?"

He moved past Kebar, said,

"*Deadwood*, love it, since Brian Cox joined, it's moved up a notch, you think?"

He tossed the box on the table, asked,

"So, you got any wineglasses?"

Kebar got a mug, none too clean, said,

"Knock yourself out."

Morronni used his silk handkerchief to clean it, poured a measure, looked at the Stoli bottle, said,

"Whatever gets you there, am I right?"

Kebar stayed standing, swaying actually, and asked,

"The fuck you want?"

Morronni pretended offense, then smiled, a predator's one, said,

"It's payday, my man."

Tossed a fat envelope on the counter, said,

"A little extra this time as we have a favor to ask."

Kebar didn't touch the thing, asked,

"And that'd be?"

"We got a shipment coming in Friday, need to know if the narcs know."

Kebar nodded and Morronni asked,

"You're good to go on that?"

Kebar gave a bitter chuckle, said,

"What you pay me for, right?"

Morroni opened the pizza box, tore off a hefty slice, stuffed his face, then midbite said,

"Slight problem has come up."

Kebar was having double vision, would he have to shoot the two Morronnis he was seeing, asked,

"Yeah, what's that?"

"Your kid, the Mick cop, he did a real number on my boy Gino."

Kebar was delighted, Jesus, that kid, said,

"And?"

Morronni was looking in disgust at his white shirt, a dab of sauce had landed there and he seemed pissed, said,

"Fucking hate when that happens, oh yeah, your boy, he's going to have to make restitution."

"What did you have in mind?"

Morronni debated another wedge and decided against it, said,

"I'll think of something."

Kebar had to know, asked,

"And if he doesn't?"

Morronni stood up brushing crumbs from his suit, said,

"Then it goes on you."

Kebar thought of the firepower he had so very close to hand and for one brief mad moment he considered blowing the scumbag to hell and gone, but then what of Lucia?

Morronni, as if he read his thoughts, laughed, said,

"You'd like to lash out, eh, show some muscle, but you know, you ain't got no fucking juice, pal, you're a cop on the take, I own your ass, and because of that little stunt, I've had to take some . . . what's the word, punitive measures, get you back in the game, it hurt me to do it but let it be a lesson to you."

Kebar went cold, asked in a very quiet tone,

"What measures?"

Morronni was at the door, said,

"And spoil the surprise?"

Then he was gone.

Kebar, despite the amount of booze he'd consumed, had become stone sober, hurting, hungover, but sober.

Time to pull out of the spiral and get his frigging act to-gether, he tore off his reeking clothes, got in the shower and stood under it, ice cold for five minutes.

It was sheer agony but it sure drove the toxins out.

Shivering, from booze and cold, he got his uniform on and was wondering if he could stomach some caffeine when the phone rang, he picked up, a tremor in his hand, went,

"Yeah?"

"Mr. B, it's Mr. Kemmel, at the nursing home."

Kebar's stomach plummeted and he went,

"What's the matter?"

Pause.

Then:

"There's been an incident."

"Stop fucking around, what happened?"

"I think you should get out here, right away."

Click.

He hung up?

Kebar was going to call the fuck right back but he better move, he threw the phone back in its cradle.

The drive out there was murder, tailgating all the way so he slammed the siren on, his own personal one he had borrowed from Property, and still took him forever to get out there, his mind a mess of snakes and dread.

He finally made it, tore out of the car, ran in and there was Kemmel, a serious expression on his face.

He motioned Kebar to his office and, biting his lower lip, said,

"It's your sister . . ."

Kebar grabbed him by the neck of his Hugo Boss shirt, snarled,

"What?"

In a high voice, Kemmel said,

"Someone got in her room, broke both her arms and, it seems, tried to strangle her."

Kebar let him go, a sob breaking from him, asked,

"Where is she?"

"At the hospital, she's at the hospital and in deep shock."

Kebar was in hell, asked,

"Did she say who did it?"

Kemmel was shaking his head, said,

"She's receded into a catatonic state, she has retreated into someplace safe in her own mind."

Kebar demanded,

"Aren't you supposed to mind the patients, isn't that your fucking job?"

Kemmel reasserted some authority, said,

"It happened in the early hours of the morning, we only have night staff, and believe you me, they're stretched to the breaking point."

Kebar got the address of the hospital and started out. Kemmel said,

"Mr. B, in light of this . . . incident, we may have to review her continuing stay here."

Kebar kept going, if he'd responded, he wasn't sure if he could keep himself from beating the schmuck to a pulp.

His uniform got him to see a doctor at the hospital without delay and he was told that she'd suffered a massive beating, her arms broken and her nose, and they were just now checking but they suspected she'd been . . . raped.

And the marks on her neck, the bruising, huge welts, whoever had done this, he'd gotten off on the strangulation, the doctor telling him this was shocked, nigh shaking.

Kebar felt like he might pass out, asked,

"May I see her?"

The doctor was sympathetic and said,

"This evening would be best, she's in intensive care now, we want to ensure there is no internal bleeding."

Back in his car, Kebar remembered Morronni's words:

"Punishment."

Lacking anywhere else to go, he went to work.

O'Brien, the CO, had him on the carpet, reamed him a new one, and warned:

"IA is on your ass, and what do you do, you take sick leave without telling anyone, you were . . . once . . . a good cop . . . but I think you better start looking at the security ads, that or Leavenworth, now get out of my sight."

He passed the kid, who was behind a desk, and tried to greet him but the kid stonewalled.

Kebar got down to the car pool and the guy assigned there smirked, went,

"Back to the Lone Ranger again?"

Kebar didn't rise to it, got in the prowl, burned rubber outa there.

His mind was hopping with every form of revenge known to man, and his first order of business was to find out who did the number on Lucia. Morronni would have contracted that out, and Kebar knew exactly who to ask.

He drove to Little Italy, went into a barbershop there, and sure enough, a bookie by the name of Lonnie was sitting in a chair, marking up the form sheets, he wasn't happy to see Kebar, who said,

"Get your ass in gear, we're taking a little ride."

Lonnie looked around for help but the other customers were suddenly engrossed in other activities, no one was going to run interference for him with the demented cop. Lonnie made a show of putting the paper aside, sighed, and followed Kebar outside. As they got in the car, Kebar said,

"That sigh you gave, hold the thought, you're gonna fucking need it."

Kebar had the radio on, not the police scanner but the C and W channel, they always played Johnny Cash and sure enough, here he was with "The Man Comes Around."

Listening to Kebar sing along with Cash, that scared the be-Jaysus out of Lonnie more than anything else, and the way he leaned on the line about a guy taking names, something very ominous about that.

Kebar took Lonnie to the same area of ground where he'd sent the kid sprawling in the dirt, pulled up, let his window down, said,

"Good spot to dump a body, you think?"

Lonnie thought,

"Oh sweet fuck."

Kebar took out his Glock, let it lie loosely in his lap, said,

"I'm going to ask you one time for some information, and if you stall, shoot me a line, I'm going to shoot you in the balls, you real clear on that?"

He was.

Kebar turned the radio off, leaned back, then asked,

"Morronni got some scumbag to do a number on my sister, the full beating and . . ."

He had to grab a breath, then:

"And . . . violated her, she's a little handicapped but she'd have known she was being hurt, now take your time, I want to know who'd be up for that type of . . . job?"

Lonnie racked his mind for some out, couldn't find one, said,

"There's a psycho, a real piece of work, that kind of . . . stuff, he loves it and if it was a retard—"

He instantly regretted using the word but fuck, he was nervous.

He chanced a look at Kebar, and no reaction save a slight tightening of his mouth. Kebar asked,

"The name and where he hangs?"

"Fernandez, he likes to go to the strip joint on Eighth and Twentieth, he's a real dangerous mother, does crystal and has a crew of some very deranged bikers."

Kebar nodded, said,

"Good, you did good, just one thing."

Then he suddenly whacked Lonnie under his chin, hard and brutal, said,

"Retard, that's a real ugly word, try and drop it, okay?"

Lonnie was seeing stars and he was fairly certain he'd had some teeth loosened. Kebar put the car in gear, asked,

"Drop you someplace?"

Lonnie, barely able to speak, muttered,

"Any subway station, any one that's near."

Five minutes later, he was getting out of the car, blood and sweat running down his face. Kebar said,

"You won't be tipping off anybody, will you, Lonnie?"

Lonnie swore on his mother's grave.

Kebar smiled, said,

"Be seeing you."

Lonnie watched him drive off and hoped Kebar wouldn't find out his mother was alive and well.

How well I have learned that there is no fence to sit on between heaven and hell. There is a deep wide gulf, a chasm, and in that chasm is no place for any man.

—JOHNNY CASH

TEN

I'M NOT GOING TO MAKE EXCUSES HERE, AS THE YANKS say, *it got away from me.*

Lucia.

The darkness had been building in my head and I liked Nora, Jesus wept, I never liked no one me whole life and she was me shot at the other life but I was afraid if I didn't get release soon, I'd go after her. Then I zoned, and I was outside the hospital, I could see meself, walking along the corridors, it was night and the dimmers were on and all I could see was that beautiful white neck, I'm not even sure if I knew who it was it belonged to anymore and a tiny part of me · was saying,

"This is a good thing, going to see the poor girl, give her a bit of company."

And then . . .

It gets all fuzzy here and next thing I was back in my car, the darkness lifting, and I was thinking of a nice place I might bring Nora for dinner.

I BEGAN TO SEE NORA REGULARLY, IT STARTED SLOW, BUT in jig time we were seeing each other about three times a week. I liked her a lot and thing is, she made me feel good about me own self and I don't want to go on about it, but her neck . . . just waiting . . . after Lucia, I was . . . what's the word, sated, she was my swan . . . didn't know exactly what I was doing . . . that's the best bit.

How rare is that?

The last thing I'd planned on was getting involved but it snuck up on me. The lovemaking was real fine and one evening, exhausted, she asked me, her head lying on my chest,

"You like me, huh?"

I smiled, said,

"Well, you're not the worst."

Then, of course, the woman's question, the one that guys hate:

"So Shea, where are we going with this?"

I had her neck in me sights but no hurry . . . right?

I said,

"Let's see how it goes."

Wrong answer.

She was up, getting dressed, said,

"Fucking guys, all the same, you call me when you know what you want."

And was gone.

I muttered the mantra of men all over the planet:

"What'd I do?"

Course I knew, I'd behaved like an arsehole . . . sorry, ass-hole.

I figured I'd give her a few days to cool off and then we'd be back on track.

Whatever track that was.

I was still riding the desk, desperate to get back on the streets. I knew Kebar was out there, doing his gig, and I missed it, and him. Whatever else, he was never boring. I was getting a cup of the burnt grains that pass for coffee with cops, adding lots of cream to kill the taste, when one of the old guys approached me, these were the beat cops, grizzled, bitter, but the very best if you needed backup, I'd been thinking of Kebar's sister a lot, something about her really twisted me heart and I was sorry, well, a bit that I'd done such a number but like I've said, sometimes it got away from me, and I'd begun buying comics, books, videos, getting a whole care package together, make it look like I was . . . *concerned*,

I couldn't believe she had lived, and too, I wanted another look at her.

The guy asked,

"Got a minute?"

For these vets, you betcha.

He said,

"Let's take it over here."

We went to an office that was crammed with files, looked like they'd never been opened, he indicated my coffee, said,

"That will rot your guts."

I put it down on the table, said,

"You don't use it?"

He laughed, went,

"Gallons of it."

He took out a pack of Luckies, a battered Zippo, fired up, coughed, said,

"No smoking here, I'm hoping they'll pension me off."

He offered the pack and I said,

"Don't smoke."

He gave a tiny smile, said,

"Stick around, you will."

I waited for whatever it was on his mind and he finally said,

"You and Kebar, you were doing pretty good out there."

I said,

"Just lucky I think."

Shook his head, said,

"Luck has fuck all to do with it, you get a partnership, they sometimes jell and make us all look good."

I asked,

"You're telling me I should go back with him?"

He crushed the butt on the floor, said,

"Kid, my days of telling anyone anything are long gone, but I figure you know about his sister?"

I said I did and how much I liked her. He took a deep breath, then told me what had happened to her.

I acted out the whole grief/shock/horror gig, asked,

"How is she doing?"

He said,

"In a catatonic state."

I asked,

"What are you suggesting I do?"

He headed for the door, said,

"Look out for your partner."

I went to the car pool but they said he hadn't come in, had called in sick . . . again.

I went back inside, found the grizzled cop, got Kebar's address and headed out there, he lived in Queens and it took me two hours to find his place.

An old apartment building, six buzzers with no names, I rang them all and finally heard his tired voice go,

"Whatever the fuck you're selling, I'm not buying."

I said,

"K, it's Shea, can I talk to you?"

A pause, then he pressed the buzzer. His apartment was on the third floor and the door was open.

The place was small, one sitting room, tiny bedroom, miniature bathroom, he was sitting on a worn sofa, dressed in a torn NYPD sweatshirt and old jeans, cleaning a gun, using oil to shine the barrel, he didn't look up, asked,

"What's on your mind?"

I said,

"I just heard about Lucia, I'm so sorry, and . . . if I can help?"

He put the gun down, said,

"I got it under control."

Dismissing me.

I asked,

"But some backup wouldn't hurt, right?"

He let out a long weary breath, said,

"Go away, kid, this gig is a no-brainer, it's a career killer, so take off, go become supercop."

I tried further.

"K, I want to help."

He finally looked at me, asked,

"What is it you don't understand about fuck off?"

I took off, stood outside for a few moments, then understood what it was I had to do.

Back at the station house, the sergeant said,

"The goon squad is waiting on you."

Fucking Internal Affairs.

I said,

"Again?"

He gave a rueful grin, said,

"Hang tough and don't forget, you can have a union rep with you."

They used the interrogation room this time.

McCarthy was wearing a fifty-dollar suit, and even at that he was robbed, I suppose it was meant to say, *This proves I'm not on the take.*

Mainly it proved he had shite taste.

The black guy was leaning against the wall, chewing on a stick, that bemused smile going, took me a minute, then I remembered . . . Rodriguez.

McCarthy indicated the seat on the other side of the table, the perp's one, and then sat opposite me, asked,

"How're they hangin', kid?"

I considered this, said,

"In a sling, I'd say, if you get your way."

He laughed, was going to be the good old boy today, said,

"I like you, kid, you have spirit and I'd hate to see you go down."

I waited and he riffled through some papers, then:

"Morronni, Kebar's paymaster, he has a sidekick, named Gino, seems somebody did a number on him."

I hadn't anything to say to this, so didn't.

He shrugged, said,

"We're not the bad guys here, kid, you take down a piece of shit, gets our vote, we can cut you a bit of slack."

Pause.

"However, you refuse to cooperate, this could be turned into a vigilante cop gig and that's not good, not good at all."

I made a show of looking at my watch, asked,

"Is there a point to this and are you ever going to get to it?"

Another laugh, less jollity this time, he said,

"A scumbag named Fernandez did a real number on your partner's sister and we know Kebar is going to take the fuck down, we want you to tell us when."

I asked,

"That's all?"

He was surprised, went,

"You'll do it?"

"Sure."

He looked at the black guy, who nodded, and then:

"Don't even think about screwing with us, got that?"

I said,

"Loud and clear."

McCarthy sat back, said,

"I'm a little skeptical at your change of attitude, what's the reason?"

I sighed, loudly, said,

"Kebar is finished, I realize that now, I don't want to go down with him."

He decided to push a bit more.

"And if we want you to wear a wire, get Kebar talking about the money, how are you on that?"

My turn to smile, said,

"I'm always wired."

McCarthy handed me his card, said,

"Call either of those numbers, let us know where and when he goes after Fernandez."

"Yes, sir."

He said I could go, his whole expression saying he didn't believe a word of what I'd said.

As I headed out, he added,

"Your fellow cops, they're not going to like you giving up your partner."

I let that hover for a moment, then said,

"Shit happens."

The black guy followed me out into the corridor, said,

"IA isn't the bad guys, think of us as the housekeeping department."

I gave him the look, said,

"Back in Ireland we call them something less flattering."

He gave me an odd look, then said in a quiet tone,

"You and me, maybe we could have a talk sometime, I think we might be on the same page."

I let that sit, then said,

"You're Internal Affairs, out to screw cops."

He maneuvered the stick in his mouth to the other side, said,

"Oh, I think, you know, you and I might be more alike than you want to admit."

I was curious, asked,

"In what way?"

He had been leaning against the wall, moved languidly off it, said,

"Lots of shit coming down the pike, gonna be a lot of casualties, and you and me, be nice if we came out on top."

I stared at him, asked,

"A rat cop, you're offering to have . . . as you Yanks say, my back?"

His cell shrilled and he began to move off, said,

"Two-way street bro, time to see which way you want to go on it."

Some guys regard a date as rather wonderful. Me . . . I don't see date *. . . I see* prey.

—Shea, in his journal

ELEVEN

I CALLED NORA THAT EVENING AND WE WENT TO THE MOV-
ies and dinner. After, we were back on line, and she
said,

"I missed you."

I was delighted, in a world getting uglier by the minute,
she was the only light I could see.

In bed later, she said,

"What's eating at you?"

I said,

"They want me to give up my partner, sell him out."

She digested that, asked,

"You have a choice?"

"Nope."

Then:

"So will you sell him out?"

"Like fuck."

She said,

"I could fall in love with you."

Wasn't as scary as I would have thought, in fact, I liked it.

A lot.

We were spending so much time with each other, Nora began hinting about us maybe living together.

I had to think about that. I'd never been in love in me life, had no idea what it was, but with Nora, I felt, when I was with her, better than who I really was and enjoyed things I never thought I'd enjoy, watching her eat, her laugh, ah Jesus, she had a great laugh, one of those reach-from-the-very-bottom-of-the-soul ones and didn't care how she looked when she was doing it.

I managed to keep that swan . . . and Lucia . . . compartmentalized . . . great term that, I learned it from Dr. Phil . . . me . . . meant you could, you know, do stuff . . . and carry on . . . regardless.

Her eyes all scrunched up, her face in spasms of delight, I could have watched that all the day long.

And she had an edge, I don't think I could ever have fallen for someone who was just . . . *nice.*

I don't do nice.

She could flay the skin off your back with her tongue and didn't allow me to bullshit or try me usual shenanigans.

A Friday night, we'd had a particularly great night, good food, great pub on West Forty-ninth Street, and just reveling in each other's company.

I took off me Claddagh band and offered it to her.

Her eyes were lit up like Christmas, she took it in her hand, stared at it, asked,

"Are you sure?"

I nodded.

She put it on, the heart turned inwards, means you're spoken for and we both knew the significance of that.

She put her hands to her neck, unclasped a chain holding a Miraculous Medal.

And believe me, it doesn't get any more Mick than that.

I protested,

"You don't have to give me something in return."

Got the look and she asked,

"Did I say I felt I had to give you something, did you hear me say that?"

No.

Like I said, a mouth on her, she put the chain around my neck, said,

"'Twas blessed by the pope."

When I'm confused, which is rarely, I get flip, protect me-self, and nearly said,

"The pope of Greenwich Village?"

Thank Christ I didn't.

With a grave expression she said,

"Our Lady will keep you safe out there on the streets."

I hoped the Lady was paying attention.

Much as I loved Nora's neck, and Jesus, I did, somewhere in me, I thought . . . no . . . not her, she might be me salvation.

She wasn't.

LONNIE WAS HURTING, BAD.

Morronni's crew had picked him up outside his favorite OTB, bundled him into a car, and taken him to a warehouse in the Bronx.

He was tied to a chair and Morronni was sitting opposite, a smile on his face.

Dressed in an Armani suit, polished Italian brogues, and a deep blue silk tie, he looked like he belonged anywhere but this rat-infested place.

Two of his crew were standing behind Lonnie. Morronni said,

"We heard you took a little ride with Kebar and it's no secret that you supply information to the cops. Hey, I'm not criticizing you, Lon, we all have to survive."

He snapped his fingers and one of the crew brought over a glass of red wine, and he took a delicate sip, made a gurgle of appreciation, continued,

"But when you fink on me, my boys, then it's . . . personal, you get my drift."

Sweat was rolling in waves down Lonnie's body, getting in his eyes, blinding him, and Morronni asked,

"Fuck, I'm forgetting my manners, would you like some vino? . . . In vino veritas, or so my priest used to say."

Lonnie croaked that he would, even his voice was shaking, and Morronni threw the wine in his face, said,

"There you go, enjoy, it's a '79 vintage, a particularly good year, smell that bouquet?"

Morronni clicked his fingers again and was handed a blow-torch, said,

"I can never quite get the hang of these things, so bear with me if I screw it up a bit."

He turned it on.

Whoosh.

A jet of flame shot into Lonnie's hair, it burned for a moment, then one of the guys doused him with a bucket of cold water. Morronni said,

"Jesus, sorry, man, I was aiming for your face."

Lonnie screamed, said,

"Tell me what you want, anything, I'll tell you whatever you need!"

Morronni was concentrating on the torch, as if he was really interested in the mechanics of the thing, said,

"Course you will, what did the cop want?"

Lonnie spilled the lot, the whole deal. When he was done, Morronni leaned over, tapped his shoulder, said,

"You did good."

Then he abruptly stood up, got a can of gas, poured it all over Lonnie, got the torch, said,

"Lemme try this one more time, you okay with that?"

As they left, one of the crew sneaked a look at the burning figure in the chair, engulfed in flame.

Morronni said,

"He's only warming up."

———

MCCARTHY AND HIS PARTNER, RODRIGUEZ, WERE HAVING
coffee as they waited for Kebar to show. They'd summoned him and he was late, fucking with them already, but that was okay, they'd some serious fucking
to do with him.

Rodriguez was contemplating another jelly doughnut,
those suckers were good but he was piling on the
pounds and had to watch it. He looked at McCarthy,
who, per usual, seemed on the verge of a coronary, the
guy was always so . . . het up. He pushed the doughnut
aside, got a match in his mouth, asked,

"Ray, ask you something?"

McCarthy was surprised, Rodriguez was Mr. Cool, hardly
ever spoke, especially in interrogations, just leaned
against the wall, chewing on a match, watching. Mc-
Carthy said,

"Sure."

Rodriguez took his time, nothing was ever rushed with
this guy, he asked,

"Why are you so stuck on this case, Kebar, the kid? I
mean, we have a shitpile of backlog stuff yet you seem
to think these are the only ones that matter, like it's
personal."

McCarthy felt his temper flare but reined it in, said,

"It is fucking personal, this Kebar, he thinks he's some
kind of cowboy, and the kid, he's got a mouth on him,
I aim to shut it the fuck up."

A sergeant looked in, said,

"Your boy is here."

McCarthy said,

"Let's bring him to the morgue first, you think?"

Rodriguez said,

"Youse de boss man."

Always riled McCarthy when he went street.

Kebar was in full uniform, his expression neutral, asked,

"The fuck you want now, don't you parasites ever do any real work?"

McCarthy smiled, said,

"We need you to view a John Doe."

Kebar asked,

"I have a choice?"

McCarthy said,

"This way. We'll even give you a ride."

THE MORGUE WAS COLD WITH THAT ANTISEPTIC SMELL that made you want to gag, a stretcher was in the center of the room, covered with a sheet, McCarthy pulled it off in one sweep and Kebar pulled back.

A charred husk of what might have once been human was curled up on the stretcher. Kebar sneered,

"Crispy critter . . . how the fuck am I supposed to know who the hell it is?"

Rodriguez spoke, startling them, said,

"We've saved you the problem, his dental records identify him as an informant named Lonnie . . . your informant, we believe."

Kebar was stunned but kept his face in gear, the world kept tilting out of focus, he said,

"You already know, why'd you bring me here?"

McCarthy got right in his face, said,

"See, here's the thing, tough guy, ol' Lonnie was last seen getting into your car, and hey, next time he shows, he's French fries."

Kebar snarled,

"Get outa my face and use your fucking head, would I waste my own informant?"

Rodriguez said,

"You might if he didn't give you what you wanted, and we know you're . . . upset, at . . . what happened to your sister."

Kebar whirled on him, his fists in balls, and McCarthy said,

"I hear she fought like a wild thing when the perp was riding her."

And he was flat on his back, a pile driver of a punch from Kebar, Rodriguez had his gun against Kebar's neck, said,

"Back off . . . now."

Kebar did, reluctantly, said,

"Pulling guns on your own, that where you guys have got to?"

He looked down at McCarthy, who was trying to sit up, spat in his face, said,

"You ever talk about my sister like that, I'll fucking kill you."

McCarthy got shakily to his feet, said,

"Assaulting an officer and making death threats, I could lock you up right now."

Kebar sneered,

"So, go ahead."

McCarthy shook his head, said,

"Give us Morronni, I'll see you do only one to five."

Kebar laughed.

"Fuck you."

McCarthy said,

"Okay, mister, play hardball but you might consider you're taking the Irish kid with you, now get the fuck out of here, start packing for the pen."

Kebar turned without a word and left.

Rodriguez said,

"Your jaw is swelling, better get an ice pack."

McCarthy rubbed his face, the pain was kicking in, and he said,

"The bastard is out of control, just where we want him."

And he smiled, despite his swelling jaw, he thought his answer was good.

He liked that.

It was . . . cool.

I BORROWED NORA'S CAR, A BATTERED PONTIAC AND what a hoor to maneuver. I'd learned to drive on a stick shift and this automatic gig, though obviously easier, took some getting used to.

And . . .

New Yorkers, not the most patient bunch, you learn as you go. I'd taken to following Kebar, if he was taking down the guy who attacked Lucia, I wanted to be there, Jesus, I had to know what he knew . . . had to.

But screwing with McCarthy was part of it.

And Lucia . . . she was the true reason.

Word was she wasn't coming back from the catatonia she'd retreated into and that made me so hot, being interrupted . . . how do they say . . . midmaneuver . . . just when I was in the zone, lost in the ice palace.

Four nights I followed him, trying to be real careful. He'd, as he'd taught me . . . *ream me a new one* if he caught me.

He'd drive to a dive on Eighth and then just sit, watching, I knew he was memorizing the players, the times they came and went, and getting a feel for the terrain.

He was going and soon, I could sense it.

And me . . . I knew Lucia had saved me from . . . like, you know . . . doing something to Nora.

Who polices the police?

— *VILLAGE VOICE* JOURNALIST

TWELVE

FOURTH NIGHT, I WAS DOZING, DESPITE THE FLASK OF
coffee I'd been sipping from, and too, Nora and I had
an active night previously. I was resting my head on
the wheel when a gun barrel pushed into the back of
my neck.

My first thought was . . . Gino . . . and I was gone.

Then Kebar's voice:

"Not too hot on this surveillance gig, are you, kid?"

He withdrew the gun, asked,

"The fuck you think you're doing, IA put you up to this,
that it?"

I said,

"Us Micks don't rat out anyone except our own people."

I heard him sigh, then he said,

"Come on, I'll buy you a brew."

We got out of the car and I clocked he was wearing all
black, combat pants, leather jacket, and sneakers. He'd
shaved his head, added to the air of menace. We headed
two blocks back, went into a bar that was marginally a
cut above the dive on Eighth. The bar guy looked like
a hardarse, asked,

"Get you officers?"

Kebar ignored the officers jibe, said,

"Maker's Mark, two, and two Bud."

He put a twenty on the counter, the guy said,

"On me, guys."

Kebar waited till we got our drinks, said,

"I want something from you, I'll ask, got it?"

He did.

Kebar left the change on the counter and we took a table,
he raised his shot, said,

"Here's to you, you dumb Mick."

Then we got to work on the Bud and he reached in his
jacket, took out a bundle, handed it over, said,

"Don't unwrap it here."

I took it, felt heavy, and stashed it in my pocket. He said,

"It's a Ruger, takes a full clip and is real fine for up close and personal."

Then he looked at me, surprise on his face, said,

"You weren't carrying, were you?"

I shook my head, Nora had asked me not to carry my police issue with me. He said,

"Christ, you are a dumb schmuck, what if something went down this evening, were you going to follow me in and use, what . . . offensive language?"

I had no idea and told him so. He stared at me and then gave a full laugh, not the bitter one he usually paraded but one of genuine amusement, said,

"You freaking kill me, kid, I dunno, are you just flat out stoopid or one of the hombres with the biggest cojones I've ever met?"

Before I could answer, he said,

"Listen up, buddy . . ."

Buddy!

"I'm going down, between IA, Morronni, the filth who hurt Lucia, there ain't no way I'm walking, and you have a real future, I 'preciate your support but it's best if you just take off."

I said,

"Same again."

Went to the bar and the bar guy said,

"Your partner is one mean dude, yeah?"

I put a twenty on the counter and he pushed it away, said,

"Get with the game."

I thought, fuckit, put the twenty back in my wallet, brought
the drinks back.

Kebar was staring at me and I went,

"What?"

His eyes were granite and he accused:

"You didn't pay, did you?"

Jesus.

I said,

"Big deal, the guy wants to stand us a drink, what's the
harm?"

He lashed out, gripped my wrist like a vise, snarled,

"Today he had you for chump change, but he has you, and
next thing, the bloodsuckers own your ass, now get
back up there, give him the goddamn money."

Fuck.

I did.

The bar guy smirked, said,

"I had you pegged for having balls, guess I was wrong."

Humiliated in about three different ways, I went back and
drained my bourbon. Kebar said,

"You want to kill some mother now? . . . Right. . . . Welcome to my world."

I stood up, said,

"You know, I was just trying to help you, but you know
what, all the damn lectures, the little homilies, I'm
sick to death of them, you have a good one."

And I stormed out of there.

Could be my imagination but I swear I heard the bar guy
chuckle.

Lucky I wasn't meeting Nora, the rage, it triggered the
urge and then . . . that frigging zoning . . . and . . .
stuff happened.

I WAS SHOOTING THE SHIT WITH ONE OF THE UNIFORMS,
leaning against our cars, grande Starbucks with an
extra shot of espresso, my hand leaning casually on the
butt of my gun, my radio squawking, I was finally able
to figure out what the hell the spew of data meant, it
was like learning a new language but one day it just
begins to make sense and you can filter out what is
relevant and what is fluff.

I felt like a cop, NYPD BLUE . . . and feck, I loved it.

Back home, being a Guard, sipping tepid tea, twirling your lousy baton, mostly you felt . . . useless.

Watching the party girls, skirts up to their arse, and then, corner of my eye, I'd see a swan do that graceful glide along the basin, such beautiful necks those creatures have.

But this, this was the deal.

The cop, looking at my hand resting on my gun, asked,

"How's that working for you?"

Cops will talk hardware all day.

I said it had a nice light weight but the trigger was sometimes liable to fold in on itself.

He nodded, said,

"See, yer Glock, the department insisted we had to keep up with the crims and carry that, but I tell you, you're chasing a perp on foot, the freaking thing sometimes goes off, blow your foot or worse your balls off, me, I carry a little extra."

Pulled up his pants and strapped to his foot, a Browning.

He drained his coffee, said,

"Our last mayor, the guys loved him, he was a no-shit guy, told the dopers, fuck you, fuck your rights, and got the streets clean, he'd have made one great pres but you know what, ain't going to happen."

Before I could hear more, I was summoned by O'Brien, who accused:

"Goofing off?"

Then added,

"You're wanted upstairs."

I figured, IA again.

Figured wrong.

O'Brien stopped outside the conference room, asked,

"You familiar with a task force?"

"Sure."

He knocked on the door and we went in. A long wooden table, lots of brass sitting round, all with stony expressions, O'Brien said,

"This is Officer O'Shea."

A tall gaunt man, in civvies, at the top of the table, said,

"O'Shea, I'm Special Agent Peters, head of this task force."

I was standing at attention, learned back in Ireland, you face the top guys, act submissive.

He said,

"Stand at ease, Officer."

I did.

He indicated a thick file, asked,

"You know anything about a strangler, traveling in Brooklyn?"

"No, sir."

He looked round at the assembled faces, then:

"Good, we're trying to keep a lid on it, prevent panic, three women to date have been strangled in Brooklyn, all in their late twenties."

He let me digest that and I asked,

"How does this concern me . . . sir?"

He bit his lower lip, then:

"Well, you're a Mick, and the killer, he's using rosary beads to strangle the women, green beads I might add."

I said,

"I didn't do it, I don't even have a beads."

He glared at me, snapped,

"Is that an attempt at humor, O'Shea?"

"No, sir."

He said,

"Reason we asked you here is, you're fresh off the boat, full of all the Mick Catholic mumbo jumbo, and we wondered if you had any input, insights into this?"

The snide dismissal of my faith rankled but I kept a lid on
it, said,

"I'd need to think about it . . . sir."

He was already dismissing me, I'd been useless, said,

"You do that, don't strain yourself."

O'Brien indicated I was to leave and he followed me out. I
said,

"I think that went well."

He stared at me, said,

"You fucked up good, here was a chance to move on up
and what . . . you get smartass . . . Jesus H."

And he strode off.

I tried,

"Sir, I'll work on it."

Without breaking stride, he said,

"I won't hold my breath."

I'd fucked up, my smart mouth doing me in yet again. I
was back riding the bloody desk and Christ, I so wanted
to be on the streets. Nothing touched the sheer rush
of that. It was the not knowing, the constant anticipa-
tion of something major. Twiddling a pencil, answering the phones, checking through traffic files, I was
bored out of me skull. To occupy my mind, I thought
about what that prick had said.

Three stranglings.

Fuck, the fourth, I'd have thought she'd be easy to find, and her neck, not my favorite, it was mottled, was sorry to waste the beads on her.

Fucking whore.

MORRONNI HAD GATHERED HIS CREW, EVEN THE SMASHED-up Gino, just released from the hospital and hurting, hurting real bad.

There was Fernandez, the psycho who'd supposedly done the job on Lucia, then the muscle guys, and others down the totem pole.

Fernandez, usually out of his head on dust, swore he hadn't done that bitch, he didn't even know where the fucking hospital was, hell, he swore, he could hardly find his way to Brooklyn most days.

Morronni said,

"Kebar, the mad fuck, has been staking out your place, Fernandez, sitting outside every night, and we figure he's about ready to take a run at you."

Morronni didn't share that he had personally threatened Kebar with retribution and although he hadn't actually got around to it Kebar, of course, had to figure it was the attack on Lucia, talk about bad fucking timing.

Fernandez, dressed in gangbanger denims and leather, smiled, three gold teeth showing, said,

"Bring it on, muthah."

Fernandez didn't give a good fuck about being accused of shit, especially if he couldn't remember it, all his life, he'd been accused of some stuff, most of it, yeah, he'd done . . . he thought.

Morronni sighed, God be with the days you could get decent help, using these off-the-wall crazies was like handling explosives, never sure when they were going to blow up in your face, he said,

"He's got backup, that Irish kid, looks like he's going to come in with him."

Fernandez seemed delighted, the mad bastard, said,

"The more the merrier, we'll be ready."

Morronni looked at him, went,

"Wasting one cop, bad enough, but two, the heat would be intense, no, we have to get rid of that Mick kid, my gut tells me he's trouble, but the K-bar, whole other story."

Gino, still seething, asked,

"Boss, I get to deal with that cocksucker, right?"

Morronni said,

"All in good time, now lemme think about it."

Then, tiring of them, he said,

"Get the fuck out of here."

The crew took off and Morronni was left with the damaged Gino, who said,

"Boss, Fernandez, the crazy fuck, he's going to be a major problem."

Morronni said,

"Him and Kebar, they'll be, how should I put it, canceling out."

Gino wasn't always sure what the hell his boss was thinking but he liked the sound of this, it sounded . . . biblical.

Other people have a nationality. The Irish and the Jews have a psychosis.

—BRENDAN BEHAN

THIRTEEN

JUST WHEN YOU'VE SETTLED INTO A ROUTINE, ALBEIT A hated one, the powers that be shake it up, shake you up.

O'Brien summoned me to his office and without any pre-amble said,

"You're back on patrol."

I was delighted, said,

"That's great, thank you . . . sir."

He gave a nasty chuckle, said,

"Don't thank me yet, you're back with Kebar."

I tried to roll with that, said,

"We've worked fairly good together, got some decent collars."

He looked at me, like, was I really that thick? Said,

"Jesus H, how dumb are you? The order came from on high and trust me, they aren't doing you no favors, Kebar is fucked, he's as good as gone and looks like they're bringing you down with him."

I had no answer to that and he barked,

"Get your ass in gear."

Kebar was leaning against the car, his head fresh shaved again, he said,

"Dead men walking."

He got behind the wheel and I waited till we pulled out before I asked,

"The fuck's that mean?"

He had two Starbucks foam cups on the dash, indicated I should take one and said,

"They're giving us enough rope to hang ourselves, we're history."

I was seriously pissed at how everyone was just wiping me off the board and asked,

"So what do we do?"

He swerved past a stalled cab, growled,

"We do our job, is what we do."

He flicked a file at me, said,

"Take a look."

It was on a guy named Crosby, a child molester, had taken two falls and was out again. I asked,

"And?"

Kebar checked his rearview mirror, said,

"He's been hanging around a schoolyard on the Lower East Side, getting ready to snatch another kid, they let this piece of garbage walk after two years, you believe it?"

I closed the file, the pictures of the kids he'd hurt were gruesome, I asked,

"What are we going to do?"

Kebar smiled, said,

"Gonna have a wee chat with him, isn't that what you Micks do . . . *chat*?"

We got to the playground and sure enough, sitting on a bench near the school was a lone figure, huddled in an army coat. Kebar said,

"He'll have a camera in that coat and candies."

I had to know, asked,

"How are we going to handle this?"

Kebar, sliding out of the car, said,

"Head-on, like a collision."

Casey watched us coming, his eyes considering flight, but he opted for defiance.

Bad idea.

Kebar said,

"They let you out, huh?"

He didn't look like a monster, but then they rarely do. He was slightly built, more like a lower-level clerk than the freak who'd done what I'd seen in the file.

He looked at Kebar, said,

"I'm cured, took the therapy in the joint and I'm all well now."

Kebar sat beside him, his body relaxed, no aggression showing, said,

"That so, then . . . how come you're hanging around a schoolyard, huh, academic interest?"

Casey was staring at me, trying to gauge how much of a threat I might be, then said,

"Just proving to myself I'm cured, that I can come here and not be tempted to . . . you know?"

Kebar looked at me, said,

"He means, he won't have to grab a kid and stick his dong in them, or what was your special gig, oh right, making a five-year-old suck your shlong?"

Casey looked offended, said,

"No need for such abusive ... language, I was sick then."

Kebar was almost smiling, real bad omen, and said,

"And the kids you fucked, you think they're all better now?"

Casey hung his head, said,

"I suffer deeply for who I was then."

Kebar reached in his jacket, took out the Glock, let it lie loosely in his lap, said,

"This here, it's a hell of a piece."

And Casey got smartass, jibed,

"You gonna shoot me, Officer?"

The mockery in his voice showed me the face he kept hidden most of the time.

Kebar said,

"You ever hear of a guy getting shot in the ankle? See, the beauty of that is, how could it be planned? Who shoots someone in the ankle? And guess what, the ankle never sets properly, you get to hobble for the rest of your miserable life."

Casey was openly defiant now, looked at me, asked,

"This guy for real?"

Kebar shot him in the ankle, stood up, said,

"Better call the paramedics, ol' Casey won't be attending school today, tell you what, buddy, I'll write you a sick note."

Looked at me, said,

"Let's roll, partner, our work here is done."

We got back in the car and I said,

"Interesting approach."

Kebar put the car in drive, said,

"My aim was off, I think I blasted his heel."

I didn't know what to say and Kebar laughed, said,

"Shitheel . . . huh?"

He was true to his demons.

—Inscription on Jim Morrison's headstone (in Greek)
by his parents

FOURTEEN

I WAS STILL HIGH FROM THE SHOOTING OF CASEY WHEN
Kebar said,

"Man, I'm hungry, let's go grab breakfast."

Like, I could eat? . . . You betcha.

We went to a diner on West Thirty-eighth and Eighth.

The waitress, who'd never see fifty again, greeted Kebar
with effusivness, said,

"Hey, hon, where've you been?'

He smiled, said,

"Keeping the filth off the streets."

She smiled in return, said,

"My hero."

I let that slide.

She asked,

"So, what can I get you keepers of the peace?"

Kebar ordered:

Two eggs over easy.

Toast, rye bread.

Link sausages.

Mushrooms and tomatoes.

OJ.

And me:

The same, the shooting, it wasn't a buzz like the necks, but
fuck, cops can't be choosers, I was cranked on the violence.

She gave me a look, then went to fill it.

Her neck was old, I hate that.

Kebar asked,

"Pedophile gave you your appetite?"

I wished I smoked, I'd have blown a cloud in his fucking face.

He changed direction, said,

"Lucia, you know, the damnedest thing, she has . . . had . . . like you saw, the mind of a child but one time, she heard Dylan sing 'Sad-Eyed Lady of the Lowlands,' man, she freaking played the song to death, that's how I see her, like that song, guess she won't be hearing it no more."

Dylan had come to Galway when I was a Guard, and I pulled crowd control.

Beautiful sunny July day and no trouble.

What I remember is this wizened gnome, crunched in on himself, singing in a croaked twisted voice.

The crowd loved him, he was sixty and he had a charisma, small as he was, a kind of radiance, and after, when we were escorting him to his car, he mumbled something that only later I realized was . . . *thanks.*

You know, that impressed me more than his whole concert.

Our food arrived and we attacked it like it was our last meal.

My coffee was bitter and seemed right.

I said,

"There's going to be a shitstorm about you shooting that guy."

He was mopping up the egg yolk with the toast, didn't
 look up, said,

"I'm going down, we both know that, so these last days I
 have, I'm going to get biblical on every sleazebag I
 can."

I couldn't keep the excitement out of my voice, asked,

"And I'm going to be with you, right, buddy?"

He reached in his wallet, laid out some bills and a very
 generous tip for the waitress, said,

"Tell you, kid, I don't give a fuck what you do, long as you
 don't get in my way."

We were outside and I had to ask,

"That means what exactly?"

He got in the car, said,

"Means, shit or get off the pot."

Cryptic, huh?

We took down a middle-ranking dealer in the Village,
 without violence, the guy knew who Kebar was, he
 wasn't going to give any lip.

Rest of the day, we issued some parking violations, adrenaline hovering above us like bad prayer.

End of the shift, I let out my breath and Kebar said,

"I get some very mixed vibes offa you, kid."

And I thought,

"If you could have seen me riding your retard sister . . ."

Before we could get into it, we saw McCarthy, the black
guy, and three other cops approach.

McCarthy was smiling, said,

"You really screwed up this time, mister, the guy you shot,
he lodged a complaint, get out of the car, slowly, you're
under arrest."

Kebar got out and they read him his rights, he never looked
at me, and they handcuffed him, I protested, went,

"Christ's sake, that necessary?"

McCarthy said,

"Shut your fucking mouth, be thankful you're not joining
him."

The black cop stayed as they led him away, and I asked
him,

"What am I supposed to do?"

He was chewing his stick, spat it out of the side of his
mouth, said,

"Get the fuck out of here."

On the way back to Brooklyn, I stopped in a music store,
bought a Dylan album, and on my third beer, I listened to "Sad-Eyed Lady."

Could only listen to a few minutes before I had to take it off, maybe if I'd had a few belts of Jameson, I'd have listened to it all, but on three lousy Millers, no way.

Reminded me of Galway, the croaks of that first one pleading with me, the rosary already in me hands.

The police never think of suspecting anyone who wears good clothes.

CHARLES PEACE, VICTORIAN MURDERER

FIFTEEN

I WENT TO SEE LUCIA, I DIDN'T WANT TO GO, TRIED TO RA-
tionalize why it would be a bad idea and then just the
hell went, thinking, if she woke, Jesus, she might remember.

The nurse on duty was a dote and said,

"She hasn't had any visitors, we thought her brother would
be by."

I didn't say he was currently in lockup and asked how she
was doing.

The nurse looked serious, said,

"She was pretty tore up, her arms broken as well as . . .
well, other violations, and she has remained comatose,
the doctors don't hold out much hope."

I was turning to go, relieved that it seemed I wouldn't be actually seeing her, when the nurse said,

"Would you like to visit?"

Fuck . . . no.

I said,

"Yes."

She was in a private room which was costing Kebar or Morronni a whole lot of cash. I was shocked when I saw her, she was attached to a myriad of tubes, her face still had the marks of bruising and her arms were in plaster. Her face looked ruined, as if she were already dead.

How far in the zone had I been? She'd looked gorgeous that night . . .

The nurse pulled up a chair, said,

"If you sit with her, it would be . . . nice."

I was thinking, rage engulfing me,

"What the fuck difference does it make?"

And as if she read my mind, she said,

"We don't know, of course, but if you spoke to her, she might be able to hear you."

Jesus.

And left me with her.

Self-conscious, feeling like a horse's arse, I faltered:

"Um, Lucia, I . . . how are you, fuck, Jesus, sorry, for curs-
ing, I um . . . oh right, I brought you Bob Dylan . . ."

And because I was afraid to stop, I rambled on about my day,
not mentioning her brother shooting a child molester but
just stuff about coffee, the city, and then about Ireland
and how one day she must come visit . . . and then I
zoned, I think I told her what a sweet fuck she'd been . . .

When I looked at my watch, an hour had passed. I stood
up, my shirt drenched in sweat, went over to her and
bent down, put a kiss on her forehead, then I was about
to leave when I stopped, reached inside my shirt, unclasped the Miraculous Medal and put it around her
neck, looked around and fuck, the nurse was standing
there, I couldn't finish . . . shite.

I couldn't help thinking as I got out of there,

"Why do people keep interrupting me with her, the night
I'd been there, an orderly had looked in, shouted, *The
hell are you doing?*"

I still don't know how I got out of there without being rec-
ognized and I gave God a bollicking.

At home they believe if you berate God, He'll seriously
come after you and with intent.

In this case, they were right on the goddamned money.

I was still on patrol but with a new partner, an old hand
name of Gillespie, who cautioned:

"I'm different from your previous partner, you hear me?"

Like I was deaf?

I said,

"Gotcha."

He went on to explain how his twenty was nearly in and he
didn't need any heroics or as he put it . . . *showboating.*

I thought,

"Yellow prick."

And that's how we played it, by the book, boring as hell
and I nearly missed my desk gig.

Nora and I were getting closer, I was able to talk to her
like I think I never spoke to anyone me whole life.
When I told her about Lucia, she cried and offered to
go visit. She wore my Claddagh ring with obvious delight, the heart turned inwards. We'd be out having a
meal or a drink and I'd notice her turning her hand,
letting the light bounce off the gold. It made me . . .
happy?

Kebar made bail but was suspended from duty, pending an
investigation and possibly a trial.

Nora and I met him for a drink and he seemed even more
ferocious than ever, his skull now completely shaven
and a dark slant to his features, like someone with a
terminal illness but who was going out with a roar.

We were in a nice bar on the West Side, the sorta shithole
where they call you *sir* with a built-in smirk. Nora had
picked it, said they did lovely food and wouldn't it be
nice to go to a smart place.

Right.

The basic truth about cops is this:

You think they ever want to attend Shakespeare in the Park? . . . Give them a diner on the Lower East Side and a battered copy of McBain, they're as content as a cop is ever gonna be.

It's called knowing your limitations or simply being true to themselves.

You know you're a cop when someone says . . . *the park* . . . you think . . . *muggers.*

Nora excused herself, went to the ladies' room, and Kebar said,

"Real nice girl, you done good."

I looked at him, the dark circles under his eyes, and asked,

"How you holding up?"

He smiled, a smile that was full of weary bitterness, said,

"This bullshit charge is going away, I had a friend of mine talk to our child molester and he realizes he was mistaken, but what can I tell you, they're making me jump through the hoops, fuck 'em."

He looked round, signaled a passing waitress, ordered a double Wild Turkey, looked at me and I shook my head. He said,

"I went by the hospital, saw Lucia had a nice medal around her neck . . ."

Then he stopped, bit his lip, said,

"Thanks, buddy."

I went American, said,

"No biggie."

He didn't look at me, said,

"Is to me."

ANOTHER WEEK OF DEAD PATROLLING WITH THE GROUCH,
we spoke little, save for him telling me how it used to
be in the good ol' days.

Yawn.

You want to alienate the young, tell them how it used to
be.

A flasher/Peeping Tom was operating in Central Park and
we got the job of flushing him out.

The damn place is bigger than Ireland.

Sure came across lots of weird shite.

Rent boys, transvestites who looked more like Hells An-
gels, desperate cases of homeless people, and of course
a whole batch of crazies.

You want to lose complete faith in the human race, troll
the park for a few hours.

We even came across a Frisbee thrower, nothing wrong there save he'd lined the Frisbee with lead . . .

Catch that.

Thursday evening, we get back to the station house and O'Brien comes racing down, said,

"Shea, in my office pronto."

I'm thinking,

"The fuck is it now?"

I get up there and he said,

"Shut the door."

He pulls out a drawer, a bottle of Paddy (jeez, I hadn't seen that brand since my old man died) and two glasses, pours lethal amounts, said,

"Get that down you."

It burned like a bastard, good though.

He let it settle, then:

"I've some bad news."

I waited, letting the whiskey shield me.

Then:

"You've been seeing a girl, named Nora . . . I um . . . she's been murdered."

I stared at him, and he continued:

"A victim of the strangler, the task force is waiting, they're going to want to ask you some questions."

I let my head drop between my knees, the room spinning, and finally asked,

"Where is she?"

"She's in the morgue, but you don't want to go there, and like I said . . . The task force?"

I was on my feet, roared,

"Fuck 'em, I want to see her."

The zoning had been bad the last few days . . . did I kill her?

He picked up the phone, spoke in a hushed tone, then put it down, said,

"Special Agent Peters is going to allow that but he'll accompany you."

I said,

"Like I give a fuck what he allows."

O'Brien said,

"I know this is a shock, but don't piss this guy off."

I stormed out of the office and ran smack into Peters, he was going to say something and I said,

"Let's go."

An unmarked car outside, two agents in it, I looked at
   Peters, sneered,

"Am I under arrest?"

He kept his voice low, asked,

"Why, you do something?"

The drive to the morgue was silent and when we got
   there, they flanked me as if I was going to run, I sure
   wanted to.

The room itself was icy, and those green walls, puke
   colored, an attendant was standing by a steel drawer,
   and Peters asked,

"You ready for this?"

"Like you give a fuck, open it."

The drawer made a squeaking noise as it was pulled back,
   and a white sheet covered the body, the attendant
   peeled it back and there she was.

Dead.

Her eyes were closed but I could see the ligature marks round
   her throat, they'd cut deeply into the skin, I stared at her,
   keeping my face in neutral and finally I nodded, said,

"It's Nora."

We went outside and Peters asked,

"Can I get you something?"

"Yeah, the fuck out of here."

Drove me back to the station and the interrogation room, Peters indicated the chair, I sat and he stood on the far side of the table, asked,

"When did you last see . . . Nora?"

"Two nights ago, I was supposed to pick her up this evening."

He watched me carefully, then,

"Can you account for your movements on that night?"

"Yeah, I was with Officer K . . . Kebar to his friends."

He had his notebook out, asked,

"You think of anyone who might have wished her harm?"

I looked up at him, said,

"Morronni, he does a number on Kebar's sister, and now, my turn to feel his rage, you talk to him, ask him for his whereabouts two nights ago or do you just hassle cops?"

He closed the notebook, said,

"Look, Shea, I understand your anger, your grief, but why don't you think this was the strangler? A green rosary was used."

I gave him my granite look, said,

"Because of one small detail, you're the expert and you missed it?"

He narrowed his eyes, wondering where I was going with this, asked,

"We double-checked everything, it has all the hallmarks of the other stranglings."

I let him wait a beat, then I said, trying not to let my voice break,

"Her finger is missing, and the gold ring I put on it."

Nothing is ever as it's supposed to be . . .
more's the Irish-ed pity.

SIXTEEN

MORRONNI WAS SERIOUSLY PISSED.

Gino, standing before him, was nervous, very.

He hadn't seen the boss this enraged for a long time and he was drinking neat bourbon, a very bad sign, meant medieval shit was coming down the pike and soon.

He stared at Gino, asked,

"The fuck were you thinking, you stupid prick?"

Gino, at a loss, asked,

"What'd I do?"

Morronni was on his feet, swaying, neat bourbon on an

empty stomach and a batch of rage will sway the best or worst of 'em, he spat,

"Do . . . fucking do, you offed the young Mick's broad, I said we'd refocus him but I didn't fucking mean for him to go ballistic and he will."

Gino crossed his heart, swore on his mother's grave, he hadn't touched her.

Morronni paused, then,

"Would that psycho Fernandez have done it?"

Gino, relieved to be off the hook, said,

"He's capable of anything."

Morroni fumed, then:

"Him and Kebar, they're gonna make a move real soon, are we ready?"

Gino, on safer ground, said,

"We have a full crew all over the club, Kebar comes in, he'll be hit from four different angles, he's history."

Morronni said,

"Make sure they're ready to go, those cops, they're gonna come real soon."

Gino smiled, said,

"They'll never know what hit them."

Morronni, back to biz, asked,

"I don't suppose Kebar told us where the cops are going to be when we make the shipment?"

Gino said,

"I think Kebar has outlived his usefulness."

Morronni said,

"Bring him down hard, you hear?"

Gino heard, loud and deadly.

Further down the street, McCarthy was briefing his troops, going,

"The kid has suffered a major loss so he's definitely going to back Kebar, they'll make their move real soon, they go in the club, let them get started and we'll go in, pick up the pieces, get most of Morronni's crew too."

His black partner was thinking,

"*Pieces* . . . bodies more like."

I WAS SITTING IN ME APARTMENT, ON MY SECOND JAMESON, trying to keep my mind a blank.

Bang on the door and I opened it, piece in my hand.

Kebar.

Carrying a large holdall.

He began,

"I'm so sorry for your loss."

I held up my hand, said,

"Don't."

He began to unpack the holdall, bulletproof vests, sawn-offs and numerous handguns, said,

"They're expecting us at the club, reason I've been casing it, let them think I'm going to go in there, and McCarthy, they're waiting too, but Fernandez, he visits a little chickie on the West Side, gets himself a bit of poontang before he goes clubbing, that's where we're going, now, you still up for it?"

I began to put on the vest, asked,

"Take a wild guess?"

We were good to go and Kebar said,

"Glad to have you on board, kid."

The duality, hell of a word that, isn't it, was in full force, I liked Kebar but I had made my plans and with regret, I sneaked a look at him, he really did see me as his backup guy, I think this is where other people feel that thing they call *regret*, I don't know about that but both sides of me were at war about my intended action.

On the way to the West Side, we didn't talk, double-checked our firepower.

The street was deserted and Kebar pointed to a run-down apartment, said,

"He's on the ground floor."

Checked his watch, said,

"He should be just about getting his ashes hauled now."

I asked,

"This is not an arrest?"

He said,

"Not too late for you to bail."

We jimmied the door with a small pick, went in real quiet and a guy was dozing on a recliner, Kebar shot him in the gut then kicked in the bedroom door, Fernandez was indeed on the job and Kebar opened up with the Magnum, a volley of shots, not much chance the lady was going to survive.

Kebar came back out, said,

"Scatter those packages of coke all over the place, make it look like a dope deal gone to shit."

Like that was going to fly.

Kebar was surveying the scene when I moved up to him, whispered.

"'Twas me fucked your sister."

His howl of anguish was cut short by the two rounds I put in his skull.

I think you can figure which side of my *duality* won out.

I had to move fast but didn't really feel hurried, I had it all mapped out in my head.

Left Kebar's car at the scene, caught the train, then grabbed a cab, had him go past Fernandez's club, saw Gino was in place. I had his apartment from traffic citations.

I had the cab drop me about five blocks from there and then strolled over. Easy to boost his door, the dumb fuck, didn't he ever hear of deadlocks?

Boy, did I get lucky, found the envelope with the picture of me accepting the money from Morronni under a pile of dirty socks.

I cleaned the Ruger, still smelled the cordite from the recent firing, and I stashed it in a rag under his mattress, and reluctantly, my last two remaining sets of green rosary beads alongside.

Hated like hell to let them go.

Walked another five blocks, then made a call to 911, reported shots from Fernandez's address.

Then I caught the train to Brooklyn, had me a large Jameson and chicken on rye, put lots of mayo on, I love that stuff, I turned on the TV and caught an episode of *Veronica Mars*, jeez, she is so hot.

I wondered how she'd look with the beads.

Turned in shortly after, man, I was beat.

Next day, all kinds of shitstorms had erupted.

I was summoned to O'Brien's office, where regretfully, he informed me that Kebar had been killed after he attempted to arrest Fernandez. As a matter of form, he asked where I was and I said I'd been home watching the ball game, this was the two hours before *Veronica Mars*.

I asked if I could see the head of the task force.

O'Brien was surprised but made the call.

Peters arrived, mumbled something about sorry for the loss of my partner, he almost sounded sincere.

Almost.

I said,

"I've been following Gino for a while and I jotted down some of the neighborhoods he was cruising in."

Peters said,

"So?"

"I checked the papers, those are the places the girls were strangled."

He chewed my arse about going out on my own and when he was done, I asked,

"You want to hear the rest or not?"

He did, begrudgingly.

I said,

"Kebar had told me Gino was always playing with a worry
beads and I didn't make the connection till the other
night when I realized Gino is Italian, he wouldn't have
a worry beads but he would have a rosary beads."

Peters was on the phone, yelling to get him Gino's address
and to have the task force suit up and get ready to
roll.

He looked at me, said,

"Sit tight, this pans out, you're in fucking clover."

I'd swear he was grinning.

Gino was charged with not only the stranglings but also
the murder of Kebar, the slugs in Kebar's head match-
ing the Ruger.

The papers went to town on it and my photo was plastered
all over, I looked pretty good, serious face, intense expression, and the mayor said I was exactly the type of
young man the department was now recruiting.

Kebar was given a hero's funeral, and in full uniform, I at-
tended. As he had no family, I got the flag, thought
that was a neat touch.

And . . . I got my gold shield.

In Kebar's apartment, they'd found tapes of Morronni's
threats and bribes and he was currently under indictment.

He'd asked to see me.

Yeah, like that was going to happen.

He claimed he had evidence of me taking bribes but none came to light.

I was given two weeks' compassionate leave for the loss of Nora and my partner and I went to Miami, lay on the beach, watched the gorgeous women, well, mainly I watched their necks, so delicate, just crying out for ornamentation.

I had to fight the urge, and the department doctor had given me some tranquilizers which I doubled up on, add a half bottle of Jameson and I could bite down, swallow hard and resist the impulse.

The odd time I thought of Lucia, and by now, they'd have transferred her to some state place.

I remembered her lovely neck and the Miraculous Medal I'd put on it.

She'd be left to rot, I figured, and then said,

"Shite happens."

No matter how I tried to summon it, I couldn't get a picture of me killing Nora and cutting her finger off, that crap would never occur to me . . . I think.

I've not got much time for the cops, but I feel sorry for them with all those violent crimes.

—BUSTER, GREAT TRAIN ROBBER

SEVENTEEN

JOE MULLOY WAS

Once

. . . a

. . . cop.

In New York.

He'd done eight rough months on the streets and it bruised him in ways he still hadn't fully come to terms with.

Staring down a guy, flying on angel dust, he had an epiphany.

His thirst for investigation was of the written kind.

He wanted to write and use words to track down the dirt.

And he wrote a semifictional account of his time, he'd had a wonderful Rilke title for the book but the publishers told him to *get real*.

And it appeared as:

Cop Out.

Jesus.

Sold modestly, *Publishers Weekly* said it had promise.

Translate as . . . Don't give up the day job.

He was still earning back the advance.

But it did lead to an offer on a small paper outside Fort Lauderdale and he honed and perfected his craft which led to a bigger paper and finally, to being an investigative reporter.

Made him a great journalist, killed his marriage.

Brooke saying,

"You're like a dog with a bone, when you're on a story, nothing else matters."

'Tis sad 'tis true.

She married a dentist two months later.

And then his beloved adored sister was murdered in New York.

A victim of the strangler.

Nora had been all lit up before this, in her weekly call, she had said,

"Met Mr. Right, not only is he a cop, he's Irish."

He'd never heard her so hopeful.

And best, the evening she rang to say the guy had given her his gold Claddagh ring.

Irish women see that as:

Signed.

Sealed.

Delivered.

Then she was strangled.

He was bereft, hit the bottle for a bit then got himself in some sort of shape and went up there for the funeral.

And that's how it began.

The Mr. Right never showed for the funeral.

The fuck was with that?

Something odd.

The guy was an Officer O'Shea and lo and behold, he was the one who cracked the strangler case.

Hello.

How convenient.

And digging more, Shea's partner was killed in a very dubious drug bust.

When Joe tried to get in touch with Shea, he learned he was on vacation.

Vacation?

His partner is killed, his girl is strangled, and he takes a holiday?

Hero cop.

The blues joined ranks, closed out questions, especially from a goddamned reporter.

And . . . Mr. Right got his gold shield.

Nora got a cold grave, his partner got the same, and Shea got to make detective.

Joe went back to his job and began to dig.

Eighteen months of solid research and he had some names to work with.

Gino.

Morronni.

Fernandez.

And a total blackout from the NYPD.

He wrote to Gino, said he was doing a book on the Brooklyn strangler and would Gino like to give his version?

A guy doing three life sentences, he'll talk to anyone.

Joe traveled up to the max security pen, brought lots of cigs and candies.

He'd been to the joint before and knew what passed for currency there.

He was put in a small room and they brought Gino in, manacled from head to toe, in a green prison uniform.

Joe said,

"Thanks for taking the time."

Gino looked like death warmed over, the prison pallor accentuated by a yellow sheen to his face.

He said,

"Buddy, all I got is time and not even much of that, I'm sick."

Joe shoved the carton across the table and a disposable lighter, the guard moved over, checked the carton and then let them be.

Gino peered at the candies, asked,

"Got any Hershey's Kisses there?"

No.

Joe said,

"Next time."

And Gino gave a smile that might have actually been tinged with sadness if he could for a moment let the tough guy persona ease.

Joe asked if he could tape the interview and Gino shrugged, hard ass back in place, asked,

"Whatcha wanna know, bud?"

Joe looked at his notes and then:

"You always claimed you weren't the strangler, any way of backing that up?"

Gino said,

"There was an incriminating photo of the kid taking kick-back from Mr. Morronni."

Joe noted how even though Gino was never getting out of prison, Morronni was still *mister.* He asked,

"The kid?"

Gino looked enraged, said,

"Young Irish cop, I trashed his place, sliced up his uni-form, and he had a hard-on for me, when the cops hit my place, the photo was gone and under my mattress, the gun that killed the kid's partner and the rosary beads . . . fuck's sake, I haven't said a prayer since I was ten years old and I ain't going to lie to you, I hurt people but never . . . never a broad."

Joe digested this, then asked,

"Any idea of who the strangler was?"

Gino said,

"The kid, he was Irish, he offed his partner, and set me up for the gig, you ever meet this kid?"

Joe shook his head. Gino said,

"Got them brooding Irish looks going for him and a kind of slow burn, but you don't get it at first, he seems harmless but then you think, there is something real cold about the dude."

"What about Morronni, Mr. Morronni, what did he think?"

Gino sighed, said,

"It was him put it together about the kid, all the kid's problems went away, everyone got wiped and he got to be a hero, very slick, I tell you, bud, I've met some real predators, some stone killers, and none of them, none of them had the iciness this kid has."

The guard moved, said,

"Time's up."

Joe stood, said,

"I'll be back soon, with the Hershey's Kisses."

Gino laughed, said,

"Better be real soon."

Before he left, Joe went to see the warden, thanked him for his cooperation, and asked,

"Gino seemed sick, is it just jail time?"

The warden looked at Joe, then said,

"Lung cancer, he's got maybe a month."

Joe involuntarily muttered,

"Jesus."

The warden said,

"I don't think Jesus has much to do with it."

JOE READ THROUGH HIS NOTES, THEN COMPARED THEM with a telephone call he'd had with Morronni.

They both sang the same song.

Joe did some more research on Shea.

In the eighteen months, he'd been to Ireland for the death of his mother and had cracked some high-profile cases, he was on the fast track to the top.

He checked the time of Shea's Irish visit and then used his search engine to check on murders there.

Shea had been in his hometown of Galway and got a hero's welcome.

Joe nearly missed it.

A girl had been strangled in Sligo, a silk ribbon used.

Joe would bet anything it was green.

He'd one last person to see, Peters, the head of the task force.

Retired six months ago, he was living in Boca, Joe got the number, said about the book he was writing and could he perhaps talk to him?

He could.

Joe drove up there, and marveled at the display of money in Boca.

Peters lived in a small bungalow off the main strip. Joe knocked at the door, he'd brought a bottle of Maker's Mark, his research had shown that Peters liked to sink a few.

He opened the door in silk pajamas, and Joe's first impression was how old he looked.

Bit like the Hef in fact but he didn't think any bunnies would be running around.

They went into a small living room, obsessively tidy, bachelors go one of two ways, let everything slide or keep it in regimental order.

Joe handed over the bottle and Peters went to get some glasses.

When he returned, he said,

"You were on the job?"

"Yeah, how'd you know?"

Peters indicated Joe should sit, as he poured healthy slugs of Maker's, said,

"You have cop eyes and you cased the place, like only a cop does."

Joe was impressed, said,

"Did eight months out of the Nine Seven."

And Peters asked,

"Why'd you quit?"

Joe thought about shining him on but the guy was sharp so he told the truth.

"I couldn't stomach it."

Peters nodded, then:

"Me, I loved it, still be doing it but I got sideswiped by a damn cab, they pensioned me out, worst day of my life, the fuck am I supposed to do now, tend to my roses?"

Joe had clocked a bare garden, not a single flower in it.

Peters drank from his glass, gave a slurp of contentment, asked,

"So, what do you want?"

Joe ran down the strangler case, Gino, Morronni, but didn't mention Shea, then said,

"I'd like to hear your thoughts on it."

Peters poured another wallop, swirled it around in the glass, as if there might be some truth in there.

If truth is to be found in the bottom of a whiskey glass,
then God help us all.

—Irish bishop in sermon on drinking

EIGHTEEN

THERE WASNT, LEAST NOT ANY THAT WOULD LAST.

Peters put it down, said,

"The whole case stunk to high heaven but we could go
with hero cop or . . ."

Joe decided to go for broke, asked,

"Gut feeling, did Gino strangle the Irish girl?"

Peters gave him an odd look, said,

"No, not his MO . . . but if my instincts are right, you're
going after Shea, be real careful, this guy is three
steps ahead of everybody else and worse, he likes to
play."

Joe stood up, thanked him for his time, and they shook
   hands, Peters didn't let go, stared at Joe, said,

"This isn't about a book, this is personal, you mentioned
   the Irish girl, you looked like you were gonna lose it."

Joe thought what the hell, he liked the guy, said,

"She was my sister."

Peters nodded, then:

"You better work on your act, buddy, Shea sees what I just
   saw, you're fucked, nine ways to an Irish Sunday and
   believe me, this guy has antennas like I never encoun-
   tered."

Joe was at the door and Peters said,

"Give me your phone contacts, I know a Guard in Ireland
   and discreetly I may be able to find out about the girl
   in Sligo, you're betting she was strangled with something green."

Joe gave him his card and said,

"Why the green?"

Peters snorted,

"Maybe he's patriotic."

Neither of them smiled.

Joe said,

"You've been a great help."

Peters laid out both hands, palms up, said, "Once

. . . were

. . . cops. Right?"

Joe took a leave of absence from his job and packed a few belongings, got a flight to Newark.

He was letting his cop experience and his journalist instincts lead him and they urged:

"Go see the sister, Lucia."

It seemed like a wild goose chase but it was just these out-of-left-field notions that had given him his biggest scoops.

He'd booked a small room in the Village on the Internet for a month. If he hadn't gotten anywhere then, well . . . fuck.

JOE HAD FORGOTTEN HOW COLD NEW YORK WINTERS WERE and after Miami, it was fierce.

He bought a heavy seaman's jacket from Goodwill, thermal underwear, and a pair of Gore-Tex boots.

He then sat down with the phone directory and began to ring the hospitals, and to his amazement, Lucia was still in the very same place.

He'd figured she'd have been shipped off to some state one long ago.

He took a cab out there, he'd rent something after this, he needed to be mobile.

He was directed to Lucia's room by a nurse who said,

"Thank God she finally has a visitor."

Joe, sensing warmth, asked,

"Would any of the nurses from eighteen months ago still be around?"

The nurse smiled, said,

"This is a very good place to work, we tend to dig our heels in here, and Maria, she still looks after Lucia, you go ahead, I'll page her."

Lucia looked like a corpse, a beautiful one but no life evident, except for the monitor that counted out her vacant moments like a death knell.

His heart felt bruised just looking at her and then he heard:

"Isn't she lovely?"

He turned to face a Spanish-looking woman, late thirties, with a face, if not pretty, certainly riveting and he felt something he'd given up on . . . attraction.

She held out her hand, said,

"I'm Maria."

He felt electricity when their hands touched and he muttered . . . "Joe."

She studied him for a moment, then asked,

"Why are you here?"

Despite his years as a journalist and the lies that sprang
naturally to him for cover, he went with some of the
truth, said,

"I'm writing a story on her brother, the hero cop."

Her face looked hurt, she said,

"His death robbed her of company and he sure worshipped
her. I thought for a while, his young partner was going
to be a regular, a gorgeous dark Irish guy . . ."

He felt a pang of . . . jealousy?

She continued,

"I saw him put a gold medal of the Madonna round her
neck and then he looked like he was massaging her
throat, it seemed . . . odd and too intimate . . . and
his face, like El Diablo, I wasn't sorry he didn't come
by no more, the feeling I had, like I interrupted
him."

Joe felt the rush, the old familiar kicking in of the story
taking shape. She asked,

"You're new to Nuevo York?"

He smiled, went,

"That obvious, huh?"

She indicated his new boots, heavy coat, and said,

"The scare effect, tourists rush out and dress like they were in the arctic."

Back in the Village, he needed to get his ass in gear, get focused.

He went to a bar near Partners in Crime bookstore and for a fleeting moment wondered about going in, seeing if his book was on the shelves.

And . . . what if it was on the remaindered shelf?

He went to the bar, ordered a Jameson and a Bud back.

Nora loved a shot of the Jay.

Used to tease him.

"Joe, can you imagine if we ever actually went to Ireland, sitting in some Galway pub, the band with bodhrans, spoons, tin whistles, playing some song to break your heart and drink, like, real Guinness?"

He downed the Jay in jig time, blot out the memories, and the bartender asked,

"Hit you again, buddy?"

Jesus, he wanted to but said,

"No, I'm good."

He had work to do.

Went to a diner and had meatloaf, gravy, mashed potatoes, and though he had no appetite, he got it down, called it . . . comfort/energy food.

Back in his room, he looked at the bare surroundings and nearly laughed, muttered,

"I've become Thomas Merton."

Yeah, Merton on Jameson.

Got his laptop fired up and did some more research on Shea.

God bless Google.

McCarthy, the Internal Affairs guy, now he might be worth a chat, he jotted down some numbers and then hit another search engine and up came the smiling face of Shea, a newspaper feature on the young hero, Joe peered for a long time at the photo and all it told him was the prick was photogenic.

Then a wave of tiredness hit and he decided to grab a power nap, just five, okay, ten minutes and he moved to the single bed, lay down and was in a deep sleep in seconds.

On his laptop screen, the smiling face of Shea seemed to watch him, the gaze unflinching and without feeling.

YOU WANT TO KNOW ABOUT COPS, YOU HANG OUT IN COP bars and if you've been on the job, they know. Joe's partner in the eight months he'd been on the force was a quiet guy named Jay, looked more like a rock star than a cop, long black hair, gray shades that he never, ever took off and despite department rules, he managed to avoid the regulation haircut, kept his hair under his cap on the job, then off duty, he let it hang.

Cops don't much like long hair, it's instinctive, but with Jay, he had enough street cred to get away with it, now if he'd tried an earring, well, whole other gig.

He didn't.

J and J they used to be called.

Joe met him in the watering hole near the Nine Six, Jay's new precinct.

Jay was dressed like an undercover vice cop. Heavy battered leather, lots of scarves, mittens, wool hat, and boots that Joe knew had steel caps.

He looked older, lots of lines around his eyes and Joe knew they weren't from laughter.

They'd been real close in the day and within five minutes, it was back to that bond.

He did a thing you don't much see cops do, he hugged Joe, said he was so sorry about Nora, Jay had always a little shine for her but his buddy's sister . . . ah-uh, no way.

They went in the bar and there was silence for one split second but then Jay got lots of:

"How yah doing?"

And drinking, talking continued.

Jay didn't ask, just upped and ordered.

"Two boilermakers."

They took them to a table, got on the other side of the

bourbon, let out a collective "Ah . . ." of serious appreciation.

They studied each other for a moment, not in any threatening way but just sussing it out, then Jay asked,

"What brings you back, bro?"

Joe felt the booze warm his stomach, let it swirl a bit, do its alchemy, then:

"I'm doing a book."

Jay signaled to the bartender for another, Joe didn't object though he had to keep his wits about him, he used to be one of them but he'd walked and that drew a line. Jay asked,

"What about?"

Joe gave him a brief outline of hero cop shit, Kebar, Shea.

Like that.

The drinks came and Joe still hadn't seen any money appear but he went with the flow, the tab would come, always did, one way or another, Jay said,

"You're full of crap, buddy."

Joe raised his glass, clinked against his friend's, said,

"Slainte."

Jay nodded, waited.

So Joe told him most of it, not all, but enough.

Jay said,

"Come outside."

For a fleeting moment Joe panicked, had he blown it already?

Outside, Jay huddled against the wind factor, got out a pack of Marlboro Red, fired one up with a heavy Zippo, said,

"I'm assuming you Florida types don't smoke, probably drink herbal tea?"

Jay's tone had a new hardness, a bitterness, and Joe tried,

"You used to be a nonsmoker."

And got the look, then:

"You used to be a cop."

Loaded.

Jay flicked the butt high into the air, a tiny flicker of light against the cold Manhattan sky and then nothing.

Jay grabbed Joe's arm, not roughly but with a certain firmness, asked,

"Cut the shit, what are you really after?"

Joe hesitated, then just spat it all out, trying to keep his voice neutral as he spoke about Shea, the stranglings, Nora.

Jay shook his head, said,

"You dumb prick, come on, we'll have another brew and I'll tell you the skinny."

The music had got louder and being a cop hangout, it was country and western, the only concession they make to sentimentality, Lucinda Williams with "Drunken Angel."

They got their drinks and Jay ushered them into an alcove, away from prying ears and where they could hear each other, said,

"You're going after Shea?"

Joe considered, said,

"Well, his name is all over this whole business."

Jay looked around, then:

"You must be out of your cotton-picking mind, bro, Shea is golden, he's so far up that corporate ladder, he's bulletproof, he's not liked but fuck, ain't nobody gonna go up against him, you do and sayonara sucker."

Joe felt a rush of rage, he'd come to his running buddy and here he was getting . . . what . . . a shit sandwich, he gritted,

"Sorry to have wasted your time, I didn't realize you'd be scared of the little bastard."

Jay was stunned, actually took a step back, calling a cop a coward, whether true or not, you better be packing more than attitude, he took a deep breath, asked,

"You hear I got shot last year?"

He hadn't.

And Jay nodded, said,

"Thought so but then, you're down there sunning yourself, why the fuck would you care what happens to
cops?"

Joe was going to say,

"I fucking care what happens to my sister."

But asked,

"How'd it happen, the shooting?"

Jay sighed, said,

"A gangbanger, fourteen years old, I took my eye offa him
and he shot me in the gut, and they're right, nothing
hurts like that sucker so yeah, it made me more careful
and I'm certainly not gonna have Top Cop thinking
I'm sniffing around him."

Joe was tired, maybe the damn cold or the series of boilermakers, he shrugged on his gloves, said,

"Sorry I took up your time."

There's always something good about seeing a copper go down. The trouble is it doesn't happen often enough.

—MAD FRANKIE FRASER

NINETEEN

JAY GRABBED HIS ARM AGAIN, SAID,

"Whoa, slow down, hothead, did I say I wouldn't help you, you hear me say that? Let's get the fuck outa here, go and have some dinner and lemme hear what you're planning."

They went to a diner around the corner, you got a cop bar, you got a nearby diner, coincidence?

Sure.

They ordered up a mess of eggs, bacon, mushrooms, tomatoes, toast, and of course coffee.

Jay said,

"You're gonna go after a star like Shea, you got to procede with caution, he gets a sniff of you, you're gone."

Joe eased on down from his rage and even ate the food with an appetite, Jay asked,

"You still listening to Van the Man?"

Joe smiled, Christ, he'd forgotten that . . . *Astral Weeks*, he'd played that like a zillion times and he remembered how much Nora loved Enya, now *that* he didn't get, all that airy fairy shit and celestial longing, the fuck was with that?

But thank God, he'd never said it to her, just acted like he was a devotee, we always lie to those we love.

Guess it's why it's called . . . an act of love.

Act as if . . .

They pushed their plates aside and Jay said,

"You want to get the dirt on the golden boy, track down a guy named McCarthy, he used to head up Internal Affairs and had a serious hard-on for Shea. Then Shea's star rocketed and word is, Shea got McCarthy smeared, the guy is working as a private dick now, his partner, a black guy, get this . . . he went to work with Shea, so much for loyalty."

Joe didn't mention he was already planning on McCarthy, said that was a great lead.

Jay yawned, said,

"Bro, I'm beat, gotta get some shuteye, here's my cell number, stay in touch and hey, be careful out there."

They'd been major fans of *Hill Street Blues*.

Outside, they did a brief hug, nothing too intimate but warm enough.

Jay watched Joe trundle off in search of the train and then he got on his cell, rang Shea, said,

"Houston, we got a problem."

WHAT A TRIP.

The past eighteen months have been a fucking roller coaster like I couldn't have planned.

Oh yeah, I planned and in ferocious detail.

Bring 'em all down.

And I did.

That shrink, back home, he'd said to me,

"I want you to act like you're a decent upright citizen and we can literally change your behavior and the mind might well follow."

Didn't I do all that good shite in the first part of this, wasn't I like a good guy?

Okay, I wasn't completely coplike, like certain things that might be . . . not kosher . . . putting the blame on that bollix Fernandez, and I have to say, that Lucia, she sure fought back.

When I went to the hospital after, put my medal round her neck, I was so zoned and had the green beads in my pocket, was going to strangle her right there in the bed but that bloody nurse was watching me.

But it worked out, kept Kebar off balance and nobody, no-fucking-body pushes me in the dirt, I knew I'd kill him right then but a little agony along the road seemed right.

When we went to off Fernandez, Kebar took me by surprise, I had him figured too dumb, he'd said before we left,

". . . I know who you really are, kid . . . what you are and the girls . . . the beads . . . I searched your place, found them green mothers but I can get you help, we'll do this thing now, and after, I'm going to bring you in, make sure you get the very best treatment."

Stupid bastard.

Like that was going to happen.

I think he cut me some slack because I was good to Lucia.

I wanted him to know that and whispered it in his ear . . . *I was the one who did your sister* . . . his howl of sheer agony before I pulled the trigger, ah, memories.

Then like freaking dominoes:

Gino.

Morronni.

McCarthy.

Brought them all down.

McCarthy's sidekick, that black guy who was always smiling, he was a whole lot sharper, he came to see me after
I screwed McCarthy, said,

"Nice work, kid."

Before I could argue, he laid it out, most of what I'd
achieved . . . I waited, then asked,

"You going anywhere with this?"

And that smile again.

He said,

"I want back in the real force, I was never cut out for this
IA snake stuff and you, you're untouchable, you can
make it happen."

I looked at him, debated, then asked,

"Why should I bring you along?"

He put a toothpick in his mouth, I wondered how it would
look in his right eye, and he said,

"This way, I don't blow the whistle on you, and with my
knowledge from IA we can go all the way."

I took the risk, mainly because I like that rush, to be out
there, on the precipice, it's the business and what an
asset he turned out to be.

Using his inside info and my status as hero cop, we were
two steps from running the department.

As for my little peccadillo, he only once ever referred to it,
said,

"Drop the green beads, you need a new act."

Cold.

Fucker could have been my psychic twin.

McCarthy I'd planted dope on, and the day he was marched out, lucky not to be doing jail time, he strode straight up to me, hissed,

"Oh you're good, better than I ever expected but mark this you sick fuck, I'm going to nail you."

My new black bro, leaning against the wall, said to him,

"Don't bang the door on your way out."

Gotta love that mad iceman.

Then the trip to Ireland, took him with me, couldn't let that sharp fuck out of my sight and I said as we arrived at Shannon,

"You're gonna love the black stuff."

The dreamy smile as he answered,

"So the babes keep telling me, white bitches that is."

Then to Galway and a hero's reception, the mayor even gave me a civic gig and I went into shy gee-shucks humble mode.

Fuckers bought it.

Managed a sideshow to Sligo and had me some there, used a silk scarf . . .

Okay, okay, it was green.

Old habits die hard, like that bitch did, die hard.

The shrinks, they want to put deep significance on the green.

Here's why:

I like the color.

What did you expect, some childhood shite where I was mistreated with something green?

Cop on.

Went to see my politico who'd gotten the green card for me, I had made sure my personal file from Templemore was sealed.

A minor incident with a woman Guard and why I'd been keen to get to America.

He was seated behind the large desk as usual but apart from a new potbelly, he seemed the same, then I detected something else . . . fear.

Oh how sweet it is.

He was scared of me.

Back in New York, I began to build on my rep, with my black angel at me back, we carved out a power base that few were willing to fuck with. The task force on the strangler had been disbanded.

Case closed.

Oh Jesus, that makes me want to laugh out loud, and that
prick who headed it up, he'd been giving me the cold
eye, I knew he was far from finished with me. I had a
little chat with my black dude, laid it out, and he said
in that sleepy way he had,

"Sounds like it's time for him to retire, let him go out in a
blaze of glory."

I liked it, a lot, asked,

"What had you in mind?"

The slow smile, then:

"Best you don't know . . . boss."

He let a trace of sarcasm leak all over *boss* and I was cool
with that, let him have his mindfuck, when the time
came, I'd show him serious mindfucking.

Gee, guess what, a week later, the task force leader got
sideswiped, and was invalided out. The profiler they'd
had, I went to see him as he was cleaning out his desk,
asked,

"Mind if I pick your brain a bit?"

I'd brought two cups of Starbucks, gave him my best choir-
boy smile. Jackson was his name and he had those eyes
that reveal nothing, my kind of guy, he flipped a thick
book into a cardboard box, said,

"Sure, what do you want to know?"

I had to tread carefully, this guy was a pro, so I said,

"I'm hoping to someday apply for Quantico and I'm fascinated by what makes up a crazy like the strangler."

He sat in the swivel chair behind the desk, took a sip of the coffee, said,

"Perfect, how'd you know exactly what I like?"

Loaded . . . right?

I said,

"Lucky guess."

He considered that, then:

"Lucky . . . maybe, I have you down as a guy who knows every move way in advance, but a guess. . . . no, guessing is not your MO."

I didn't like the MO crack but winged it, asked,

"So?"

He put his hands behind his head, Mr. Laid Back, said,

"Gino . . . the guy they put away for this, he doesn't fit the profile I'd drawn up, the guy I outlined is a sexual sociopath, completely lacking in empathy, or indeed any of what we call human emotions, but like all sociopaths, you'll find he's utterly charming, on the way up in . . . whatever career he's chosen . . . and very very dangerous . . . he'll kill again . . . and again, he's unable not to."

He was watching me closely.

Maybe he might have to have a little drive-by his own self.
I asked,

"But what spurs him on, why is he for example . . .
using . . . rosary beads?"

Jackson smiled, said,

"You tell me."

Jesus.

I reined in, asked,

"What?"

He said,

"You want to get into this field, now's your chance, give it
a shot."

Minefield.

I said,

"Some religious nut, ex-priest maybe."

His eyes closed for a minute, then he said,

"Hmmm . . . I'd hazard a guess it's something deep buried
in his childhood, a childhood trauma, connected to
the rosary, and his rage, suppressed for so long, uses
the symbol of his . . . hurt."

I couldn't let that sexual sociopath slur go, I knew I should
steer clear but fuck, I asked,

"You're sure he's a sexual . . . whatever you called him, couldn't he just be one highly intelligent individual . . . playing with the cops?"

He stood up, said,

"You know better than that, and the one thing I know for sure, this guy, he's a deviant, a predator of the worst sexual type."

The fuck was playing with me, I'd swear it, but I'd lost the control, and that never . . . fucking never . . . happens, so I said,

"Thanks for the help."

I was at the door when he said,

"You didn't touch your coffee."

I paused, said,

"I guessed wrong on my own taste."

I might be wrong but I think he sniggered, he said,

"Shea, you don't mind if I call you that? . . . The one thing you're sure of is exactly what you like."

A Private Eye?

TWENTY

JOE HAD NO TROUBLE FINDING MCCARTHY, HIS OFFICE where he operated as a private investigator was in the yellow pages, the address on the Lower East Side.

Joe took a cab and the building was run-down, with other listings for Realtors, a tanning studio, and pet grooming.

All the winners.

He went up two flights of stairs, the elevator was out of order, and McCarthy's office was closed. Joe knocked a few times and an adjoining door opened and a tired-looking guy in shirtsleeves asked,

"You looking for Mac?"

"Yes, yes I am."

The guy gave Joe the once-over and asked,

"You're not collecting rent or shit?"

Joe indicated his working gear, said,

"I look like a guy who collects rent?"

A shrug, then the guy said,

"Mac will be in his real office, the tavern two blocks down, called Happy Times."

Then he gave a bitter laugh, said,

"Whatever else, happy it fuckin ain't."

Joe said,

"Thanks for your help."

The guy stared at him, said,

"For what, I never saw you, got it?"

He got it.

Then got out of there.

The Happy Tavern looked like the last stop before the street, welfare people being the main clientele and a real nasty piece of work riding the pump, Joe ordered a draft, thinking coffee wouldn't be a wise choice, and the guy spilled most of it on the counter, said,

"Five bucks."

Joe put the five on the counter, added a buck and the guy grunted, said,

"Last of the big freaking spenders."

Joe took the brew, looked around, noticed a man near the window, a shot glass empty in front of him and the sports page open, he had a stub of a pencil and was marking the page with a halfhearted focus. Joe approached, asked,

"Mr. McCarthy?"

The guy looked up, his eyes fucked from booze and desperation, he croaked, his voice a ragged choke,

"Who's asking?"

Joe needed his attention, said in a low voice,

"A guy who might be able to get Shea."

And it seemed as if the guy's eyes actually cleared a little, he said,

"Get me a bourbon, we'll talk."

Joe didn't ask if he had any particular brand in mind, he got that and more surliness from the bartender, brought it back, put it down on the table, McCarthy motioned for him to sit, he did.

The bourbon had brought McCarthy back to temporary life, he said,

"You were on the job?"

Joe nearly laughed, they always could tell, he asked back,

"You're using the past tense, why d'you think I'm still not a cop?"

McCarthy sighed, the glass nearly empty already, said,

"You have the eyes but not the edge, least not anymore."

Joe was going to say,

"That's a fucking bit rich from a has-been, staring into a whiskey glass."

Went with:

"I'm doing a book on the case. Any insights you might have?"

McCarthy shot back,

"No you're not, doing a book, this is some personal gig, I spent ten years in IA and one thing I know is a goddamn lie when I hear it."

Joe figured the easy way wasn't going to work, the guy was beyond bitter so hard-ass would be the only route, he asked,

"Why'd you quit?"

McCarthy made a sound that was between a groan and a snigger, said,

"They got me out, well, Shea, the fucking golden boy and my own backup guy, dumb fuck I was, I never saw them coming, but I'll tell you something, my partner,

Rodriguez, it's my feeling he never left IA. He's up close and personal with Shea but my gut tells me, he is still IA. I thought I'd be able to get Shea, but like I said, I never saw him coming."

Then he looked at Joe, said quietly,

"And neither will you."

Joe said,

"You don't know me."

McCarthy began to roll the empty shot glass, said,

"I know them."

Joe figured he wasn't going to get any useful information and got ready to leave, he put a twenty on the table, said,

"Have another on me."

McCarthy ignored the bill, asked,

"You got any friends still on the force?"

Joe debated, then told him of his ex-partner, Jay, and he could see McCarthy rummage through whatever mental faculties he still had, then:

"Yeah, I know the guy, one of Shea's crew."

Joe was stunned, protested, said,

"Uh-oh, not Jay, you're way off the beam there, buddy."

McCarthy gave a grim smile, said,

"Try finding any of the young Turks not in Shea's pocket, now that would be a short book."

He stared into space for a minute, then warned,

"Be smart, drop it, you're no match for these guys."

Joe stood up, said,

"I'm a little surprised at a guy like you."

McCarthy came a little back to life, looked up, and Joe said,

"You were the head honcho in Internal Affairs and you just packed up your tent, went and hid in a goddamn bottle of bourbon, thought you guys were supposed to be relentless, what the fuck happened to you?"

McCarthy said,

"They let me live."

JOE WAS RATTLED BY THE WHOLE MAGNITUDE OF WHAT he hoped to achieve, bring down a hero cop, and to keep his mind from freaking out, he indulged in a fantasy, about the nurse, Maria, here's how he saw it go down.

He'd ring the hospital where Lucia was and ask if he could speak with Maria, he wasn't sure exactly what good this was doing him, this pie in the sky scenario but it felt good, she'd come on the line and he'd explain who he was, she'd say,

"I remember you, the tourist to New York."

But say it with warmth, and encouraged, he'd ask,

"Might I take you to dinner?"

Couldn't believe he was asking, and if only in reality he
could do that. He imagined she'd laugh and he'd like
that laugh, it would come from deep within, he could
almost see her face, she'd say,

"Not so much a tourist now I think, I would love to."

He'd arrange to meet her in midtown and they'd have a
drink then do dinner, she'd say that would be lovely.

Lovely . . . if only, and he realized he was projecting his
sister's personality on the nurse.

His hands were sweating, it had been a long time since
he'd asked anyone out and certainly since Nora's death,
it had never even crossed his mind. He did know this
whole mad fantasy wasn't really helping.

And then the guilt, the fuck was he doing, even thinking
of dating? He was supposed to be tracking a killer and
then he thought,

"I'm even more stressed than I thought."

Instead of making the dream happen, he finally rented a
car, a Pontiac, he'd always wanted one of those.

The rest of the day, he was edgy, veering between excitement and he had to admit, fear.

He studied his notes on Shea, work always calmed him.

Finally, he went out, hit a local bar, stopped the useless daydreams.

THE MEETING WITH MCCARTHY HAD DEPRESSED JOE more than he liked to admit.

After, he headed back to his place, he was bone weary, information overload, he hadn't liked McCarthy but he sure hated to see a man's spirit crushed. He was bothered too by the implication that Jay was in Shea's pocket . . . could that be true?

Joe was no longer a cop, and it did make horrible sense that Jay was going to lean toward cops, not civilians.

He knew he should eat something but he was wired and needed to just climb down a notch from the fevered speculations of his mind.

A little weed would do that but reading always helped too.

His staples, the books that had influenced him most, were sitting on his shelf, dog-eared, underlined, held together by tape.

Michael Herr . . . *Dispatches.*

Pete Dexter . . . *The Paperboy.*

Michael Connelly . . . *Crime Beat.*

He opened the Herr at random and hit on the disappearance of Sean Flynn, Errol's son . . . it saddened him so.

He closed the book and figured he'd done most of his

groundwork, time to confront the beast, see if he could meet with Shea.

All he'd heard, read, researched on the guy and still, he didn't really have a handle on him, the guy was like a ghost, there was a ton of data but no substance.

He'd call, give the line about the book etc. and see if the guy would meet him.

If he was, as seemed to be the scenario, a narcissistic personality, he wouldn't be able to turn down the chance to talk about himself, and if Jay had tipped him off, then they'd have themselves a hell of a mental game of chess.

Joe moved to his narrow bed, lay down, thought about Nora, and his heart burned in his chest, if that smooth son of a bitch had strangled her, by Christ, Joe would bring him down.

It was no longer anything about a story, or a book, it was purely personal.

And the black guy, who'd deserted McCarthy, hooked up with Shea, now there was one fascinating character.

Shake hands with the devil.

TWENTY-ONE

COULD A GUY BE THAT RUTHLESS, THAT CALCULATING?

Everything in Joe's experience told him that here was the real dangerous one, the guy who smiled and you took your eyes off him.

Death row had currently three of these smiling charmers, and the one thing they all had in common, they managed to somehow get behind you, you never actually got to meet them head-on, and that was the biggest mistake of all, letting them out of your line of vision.

Joe set his cheap alarm clock, be up early and on the phone, he felt that rush of adrenaline that said,

"We're racing to the conclusion."

He wondered if he still had what it took for the game, McCarthy's gibe that he'd lost his edge rattled.

He'd know soon enough.

His dreams were troubled, Shea in a Nam jacket, the music of Hendrix blasting behind him, and a black figure, in the smoke, never quite emerging but oozing malice and menace . . . Nora was right there, saying in Irish, *Sin scéal eile* . . . that's another story.

He was up way before the alarm, felt the cold seep through his bones and figured he'd been too long in Miami. He wondered anew how he'd tramped those same streets for eight months, he brewed some coffee, at least the damn sparse room had that, and grabbed a fast, tepid shower, then dressed for warmth. Poured his coffee into a mug that held the logo:

CHRISTIANS ARE DOING IT FOR THEMSELVES.

He muttered . . . *duh?*

He sat, sipped at the steaming coffee and took a bite out of a stale doughnut, cop legacy.

Read through most of his notes and then the doubt surfaced, as it always did, was he up to it?

How would it be if he got face-to-face with Shea . . . the guy who'd more than likely strangled his sister . . . and his hands began to shake?

He said,

"Fucking marvelous."

Shea, to see a tremble in his hands, that would be just hunky dory. He suddenly remembered a visit to a death row inmate, some five years back, the guy had been convicted of murdering three children in a horrendous fashion and was due to be executed in two weeks. Joe had been corresponding with him for over a year, doing a series of articles on the last weeks of death row inmates. The guy, named Sutton, had finally agreed to see him.

Joe, a prison pro by then, had brought along the requisite candies, smokes, and gum, those guys loved to chew.

Sutton had been led into the room in manacles, the orange jumpsuit and two guards along. Took him a moment to get seated due to the chains, then he stared at Joe, asked,

"How yah doing?"

Joe was thrown, rallied.

"Um, pretty good."

And barely stopped short of asking him how he was doing.

Jesus.

Joe pushed the goodies over and Sutton nodded, said,

"These homies gonna be firing me up in a few weeks."

Joe could never be sure but it seemed as if a smile passed between the guards. He took out his recorder, asked if Sutton minded and as long as he lived, he'd never forget the smile on Sutton's face as he said, in a very friendly tone,

"Do whatever you gotta do, bro, but trust me on this, you ain't never gonna forget this here . . . chat."

Joe, going by his usual rote, asked,

"How's the clemency plea progressing?"

Sutton, a smile curling on his lip, said,

"You been misinformed, hoss, else you ain't done your damn homework."

Joe, flustered, angry too, had he screwed up? Tried:

"They've turned it down?"

And Sutton let out a thin laugh, not like any laugh Joe had ever heard, more like a thin dribble of hysteria, said,

"I didn't apply for no clemency, hoss."

And Joe, like an idiot echo, went,

"You didn't?"

Sutton, with some difficulty, turned around in his seat, looked at the guards as if to say,

"You believe this shit?"

Then back to Joe, said,

"I done killed those kids, why in tarnation I be seeking mercy?"

Joe, accustomed to pleas of innocence, angry rebuttals, said,

"You don't deny it?"

And got that horrible mockery of laughter again, Sutton said,

"Damn straight, not only did I kill 'em, I enjoyed it and gimme a shot, I'd be out there, doing 'em all over again . . . Fire me up another smoke, hoss."

Joe had forgotten all his journalistic distance, his honed skills, simply asked,

"You . . . enjoyed . . . hurting . . . children?"

Sutton stared at him, then said,

"You better get a grip, hoss, you hope to stay in this line of business, it's who I am, what I am . . . I fess up . . . but you, mistah . . . who are you?"

Then Sutton shouted to the guards,

"Git me the hell outa here, this guy is some kind of amateur night and I'm missing *American Idol.*"

One of the guards whispered to Joe as they left,

"You sure you're cut out for this line of work?"

Joe learned from that, learned well, cut yourself off from the task in hand, it's a job, you're a pro and do it . . . professionally.

When Sutton was executed, Joe drank three shots of Jameson to mark each of the three children and said as toast to Sutton,

"May you roast in hell."

And meant it.

*The private terror of the liberal spirit is invariably
suicide, not murder.*

—NORMAN MAILER

TWENTY-TWO

THINGS HAD BEEN GOING SO WELL, I'M IRISH, I SHOULD
have known that shite was coming.

Rodriguez seemed to have his lazy smile in place all the
time and I asked,

"What's with the smile, you know some private joke I
don't?"

He was chewing on that damn stick as usual and he said,

"Lots of jokes you don't get, boss."

The fuckhead, one of these days, I'd see about cashing in
his chips, I smiled back, asked,

"Try me?"

He moved off from the wall in that languid way he had, said,

"Naw, it's more like a black thing, you dig?"

It had been his idea to recruit cops from different precincts, unofficially of course, get a network in place, throw some payola their way and cover our arses. I got a call from a guy down in the Seventh, name of Jay, took me a moment to figure out who he was and as I did, he said,

"Houston, we got a problem."

Jesus . . . cops.

I said,

"Spit it out."

He told me about a journalist who was reinvestigating the strangling and the whole Kebar scenario, claimed he was doing a book. I wasn't concerned, journalists came at this every so often, I'd meet with them, give them my neon charm and apparently access to all areas, get their endorsement, truth is, I kind of enjoyed it, fucking with these hotshots. Jay said,

"This guy used to be on the job, was my partner for a time."

Now, I relaxed, ex-cop, perfect, I said,

"No biggie, what's your problem?"

He paused, then:

"He's Nora's brother."

Took me a moment to get it, then kept my voice level and asked,

"So?"

"He wants to meet with you, I thought you should be prepared."

I glanced up at Rodriguez, who was definitely interested, then said,

"I'd be glad to meet with him, any relation of Nora's . . . makes him, like, family."

Yeah, like dead family.

Then Jay said,

"He won't know you know who he is."

I focused, then said:

"Thanks, Jay, and we may have something real sweet coming your way."

He protested,

"There's no need, boss, I just wanted to keep you in the frame."

Dumb fuck, like there was a cop on the planet didn't want something, I said,

"Consider it an early Christmas bonus."

And hung up.

I outlined the call to Rodriguez, who mulled it over, then said,

"Let him come on in, see what he's got."

I said,

"Why the hell not."

Rodriguez took off to do some background on the journalist, one of his real talents is finding dirt.

THE JOURNALIST'S CALL CAME IN JUST BEFORE NOON AND he sounded affable, laid-back, shooting me the line about his book, and would it be possible to have a meet, get my take on the whole saga?

Jesus, he was full of it.

I was equally smarmy and said,

"I'm always available to the press and hey, I'm having lunch in an Irish pub on Park Avenue and Thirty-eighth . . . you want to join me, we could do a relaxed interview, you guys like the odd brew, am I right?"

That would be terrific, he agreed.

I was tempted to wear the dress blues but opted for the casual look, show I was an easygoing guy, wore a heavy parka over an old sports jacket, chinos and Timberland boots to navigate the footpaths. I buzzed Rodriguez, told him to drop by around one thirty, get a feel for the guy.

On my way out, I met the chief, O'Brien, and man, how the balance of power had changed.

I'd been the new kid, him the old wise rabbi, laying down
the rules. When all the stuff had gone down, he lost
the plot, too much happening for him to grab hold of.
He knew he'd been sandbagged, fucked over, used and
abused, and he didn't know then, that was only the
opening act.

Suddenly, I was golden and he was plain confused. Rodriguez found out that O'Brien had a wee fondness for
young girls so we set him up with a twelve-year-old,
sure, she looked more but we got the pictures and I
laid them on his desk one bright Monday morning,
said,

"She's twelve."

His face had been ravaged, and he looked at me with fear
and loathing, asked,

"What's the deal?"

And I leaned over, finally getting to patronize the fuck the
way he'd done to me, said,

"Old man, don't fuck with me, you'll be fine."

As I went to leave he asked,

"That's it, you've nothing else to say?"

And I gave him my best charismatic smile, said,

"Don't dip it in young honey."

Now, as we met, he avoided my eyes, said,

"Detective O'Shea."

I reached in my pockets, took out some tickets, said,

"My dry cleaning, I forgot to collect it, be a sweetheart will you?"

My mobile, sorry, cell, rang as I went to call a cab, I could have pulled a car from the pool but if I was going to have a brew? . . . I answered . . . Rodriguez, who asked,

"You good to go?"

"Sure."

Then he surprised me with:

"Are you nervous, this guy has a hard-on cos of his sister?"

I laughed, told the truth.

"I don't do nerves."

A pause, then:

"Probably best not to run that quote by the journalist."

I got to the pub and Mick, the owner, all glad handshakes and shite, I'd gotten him out of some serious stuff with health inspectors and plus, having a cop frequent your joint was damn fine protection so he led me to the best table, at the back and secluded, asked,

"And you'll be having a drink to start?"

"Pint of Harp, I'm waiting on someone and we'll order the grub when he gets here."

He was hovering, what? . . . Like I was going to tell him who I was expecting? He said,

"We've some grand fresh salmon just in and if I might recommend . . ."

I gave him the look, said,

"The Harp?"

"Oh right, I'll send the girl right over with a pint fresh off the barrel."

He had a daughter, Molly or one of those real Irish names, she had that neck I liked and

I'd been thinking . . .

Been a while since . . .

Then the Pogues came on the speakers and for some odd reason, I remembered the Dylan CD I'd bought . . . for Lucia or Nora? Fuck, I couldn't recall. This had been happening to me more often, I got like a blank in my mind, couldn't pin down details which is one of the reasons I've been writing stuff down . . . called it my glitch, a breakdown in transmission. I wasn't too worried, when you'd come as far as I had in such a short space of time, there was going to be fallout . . . right?

I'd have liked to have known though which of them had me Miraculous Medal.

The only thing that truly bothered me was Nora, I'd liked her, really felt there was a chance I might move past all this darkness, and killing her, I never planned that and truth was, I couldn't recall one single detail of it but that sometimes happened.

A waitress in her twenties came with the Harp, said,

"That will do you good."

A pint of carbonated crap, whatever else it would do, good wasn't going to be part of it.

A different song had hit the speakers and she asked,

"Like it?"

It sounded familiar, sort of, I said,

"I dunno."

She said, triumphantly,

"It's Bono with Green Day."

The fuck he wanted to do that for?

I said,

"Different."

She was still hovering and I asked, with just a hint of edge,

"Was there something else?"

She didn't like it and I felt better.

I saw a guy weave through the tables, dressed for serious

weather, and he spotted me, came over, pulled off his heavy gloves, asked,

"Lieutenant O'Shea?"

Got my rank wrong but I let it slide, said, taking his hand,

"Call me Shea . . . it's Joe . . . right?'

I indicated for him to sit, asked what he'd drink.

"Sparkling water."

I needled a bit, asked,

"Nothing stronger?"

He shook his head and I got the water for him, said,

"Us Micks, we find it hard to pay for water."

He was pulling out a tape recorder and asked,

"You mind ?"

I was still in my Mr. Nice Guy phase, said,

"Long as you don't mind Green Day on there."

I suggested we get the food ordered and then we could eat and talk. I ordered a steak, mashed spuds, and he went for a lightly grilled cheese sandwich. We bullshitted about the weather till the food came and then he hit the start button, said,

"Okay."

First five minutes, he asked about my career and my mete-
oric rise, I played the humility card and his sandwich
lay untouched, I'd gotten half of my steak put away, I
fucking love meat.

Then he got sharper, asked,

"It must have been a rough time for you then, losing your
girl, your partner?"

I pushed my plate away, as if I'd lost my appetite, said,

"It's beyond comprehension, even now."

He used a knife to cut his sandwich but still didn't eat,
then hit with:

"You didn't attend the funeral, your girl's I mean?"

I stared at him, asked,

"How do you know that?"

He made a show of rummaging through a battered notebook, then said,

"Yeah, says here, you were on . . . lemme see, on vacation,
in Florida?"

I drained my pint, decided to up the ante, said,

"I was hurting, they gave me compassionate leave and seeing . . . as you call her, my girl . . . being put in the
ground, I couldn't face it but what's your point, why is
it relevant to . . . a story about my partner?"

He was going to try subtle hardball, well, fuck, back at you.

He said,

"Just trying to get an all-around picture of the whole event."

I pushed a bit more, said,

"You once were a cop?"

He was taken aback, said,

"Yes, for about eight months."

I debated my next question, then went for it.

"Couldn't cut it, huh?"

And saw the flash, and Jesus, for one brief moment, it was like Nora, the same eyes, before he could respond, I said,

"You remind me of someone, we ever meet before?"

He shook his head, he seemed to have lost his gangbanger tone and said simply,

"I'd remember."

The owner came over, asked if everything was satisfactory, eyeing the untouched sandwich, and Joe said,

"An espresso would be good."

I said,

"Me too."

Then I leaned back, said,

"You haven't asked me about my partner, wasn't that the focus of the . . . *book*?"

He rallied and asked me some general stuff and we breezed through that, then he said,

"If it's okay with you, I'll type up what I've got, let you have a look, see if it sounds right, how would that be?"

I said,

"Sure."

His whole attitude had altered, a barely suppressed rage was building in him so I thought I'd see if I could bring it out to play, I said,

"Off the record Joe, Nora, my girl . . . ?"

I let the name sting him, then:

"I found out after, she was giving it away all over Brooklyn, a tramp in fact . . . or as one of the guys said . . . a cut above a ten-dollar whore."

He looked lashed and I indicated his sandwich, asked,

"You lost your appetite?"

His notebook had been put aside and his fists were clenched, he said,

"I think we're more or less done."

He was on the brink so I upped the ante, said,

"I can get a doggie bag, you could have it later, you know, when you're typing up your notes."

He looked at me then, and pure hatred blazed from his eyes, he took out his wallet.

And I went,

"My treat, let the NYPD treat one of its former officers."

He threw a bundle of bills on the table, said,

"I don't think so."

He stood up, I didn't and I said,

"You'll lemme see those notes, right?"

He nodded, then reached in his jacket and for a crazy moment, I wondered if he had a piece.

He withdrew a small paper bag, chucked it on the table, said,

"Thought you might be needing this."

And he was gone.

I waited a moment, then opened the bag and out spilled:

A green rosary.

KILLING TIME

TWENTY-THREE

JOE WAS FURIOUS WITH HIMSELF, HE'D LET SHEA GET TO
him and he'd lost his cool and the rosary beads, now
that was just stupid, he'd found it in one of those arty
stores in the Village, it felt good but it was dumb.

Way fucking dumb.

Talk about blowing your cover.

And now, Shea would come after him.

Guaranteed.

The fuck had a way of getting rid of people and looking
good at it.

Joe even glanced over his shoulder, paranoia growing by
the minute.

He hailed a cab, the damn Pontiac he'd rented wouldn't start that morning, had the cab take him to Battery Park, cost a bundle but hey, so it goes.

Cameron, an ex-heist guy, hung out there, and Joe, Joe had let a beef with him slide and Cameron had pledged:

"You ever need a favor . . ."

He needed a gun, that was a favor . . . right?

Took him a time to locate Cameron but after an hour, he got him in a coffee shop, and Cam went,

"No shit, the cop, where you been hiding, buddy, heard you took early retirement."

Cam looked old, deep lines under his eyes, and his skin had that gray look of someone who's either indoors too much or sick or both.

Joe got an espresso, and they shot the breeze for a bit till Cam asked,

"So, what do you want, Joe? I'm glad to see you, well, a bit anyway but you didn't come all the way over here to see how I was doing."

Joe cut to the chase and Cam protested for a while, not in the biz no more, snow job.

Joe stopped him with:

"Cut the crap, you owe me, I'm calling it in."

Cam sighed and said,

"Come on."

Led him a block away to where his battered Chevy was
parked and said,

"Don't suppose you can fix my parking tickets?"

Got the look and laughed, said,

"Can't blame a guy for trying."

They got in the front and from under the seat, Cam pro-
duced a McDonald's bag, opened it, the smell of fries
and burgers emanating, took out a Glock, and a clip of
ammo, said,

"Just like you guys carry on the job."

Joe took it, asked,

"Is it clean?"

Cam laughed, said,

"We at McDonald's pride ourselves on our hygiene."

Joe reached for his wallet and Cam said,

"Give me a hundred bucks and we're even."

As Joe got out of the car, Cam said,

"No offense but don't come down here no more, cops
aren't real popular."

Joe said,

"Ex-cop."

He was closing the door when Cam added,

"Once a cop . . ."

It was late when Joe got back to his room, he got inside, turned on the light and nearly had a heart attack.

Sitting on his bed was a black guy, chewing a match, looking relaxed, a lazy smile on his face, Joe had the Glock in his jacket but he hadn't loaded the sucker.

Fuck.

The guy said,

"Sorry for startling you but we need to talk, I'm Rodriguez."

Joe was sure this was it, Shea had sent him to do the job, and as if reading his thoughts, the guy said,

"I'm here to help you . . . help you get Shea."

THE GUY REACHED DOWN, PICKED UP A BROWN PAPER bag, asked,

"You drink Wild Turkey?"

Joe got his mug and a water glass, handed them over and then realized, said,

"You were Internal Affairs?"

Rodriguez poured freely, handed the mug to Joe, said,

"Wrong tense."

"Excuse me?'

"Am Internal Affairs, never left, it was a snow job to get Shea, hell, he even believed I had Peters sideswiped, pure accident, a situation we took advantage of to get me tight with Shea, we've been planning this operation for nearly two years, we know Shea is the strangler, but no proof, and we're going to bring down a shitload of cops with him, he's got them in his pocket."

"Does McCarthy know?"

Rodriguez sighed, said,

"No, he's a drunk, how it goes."

Joe took a deep swallow and the stuff burned, he was trying to bite down on his anger, asked,

"You knew this guy was killing women and what, you've had your finger up yer ass, waiting for what, him to do it again?"

Rodriguez stuck another match in his mouth, said,

"I understand your anger."

Joe nearly went for him, said,

"The fuck you do."

Rodriguez took it with that slow smile, said,

"I've been on the guy, 24/7 . . . hell, I even went to Ireland with him."

Joe put the mug down, lest he fling the contents in Rodriguez's face, asked,

"And when he took out the girl in Sligo, were you on him . . . 24 fucking 7?"

Rodriguez let out a low whistle, not easy with a match in your mouth, said,

"You're good, did your background, but he got away from me, this guy is the iceman, the ultimate predator, but we have a shot at him now."

Joe reached for the bottle, poured, asked about the shot they had at Shea now.

"Yeah, how's that?"

Rodriguez leaned against the wall, almost a lazy pose, said,

"Lucia, his partner's sister, he tried to off her but got interrupted, now if she were to come around and identify him?"

Joe stared at him, said,

"I don't think that's too likely to happen."

Rodriguez gave the lazy smile, no warmth, said,

"But if he thought she had?"

Joe suddenly got the gig, said,

"And I'm the guy to tell him?"

Rodriguez said,

"He killed your sister, don't you want to bring him down?"

Joe said,

"You're IA . . . like I'm supposed to trust you?"

Rodriguez filled his water glass but the booze seemed to have little visible effect on him, said,

"And what do you call your partner, Jay, right . . . who sold you out to Shea . . . you think he's better than me?"

Joe lost it, near screamed,

"He's a treacherous son of a bitch."

Rodriguez looked at him, said,

"There's that I guess."

If you police an armed society, you learn to shoot first or you're dead.

—Chief Constable John Alderton

TWENTY-FOUR

I WAS SITTING AT ME DESK, A STARBUCKS VANILLA-
flavored latte before me and the frigging beads in me
right hand.

Where did he get it?

And, as if on cue, the phone rang, I picked up, heard,

"Lieutenant Shea, we may have a major break in the case."

The fucking writer.

I kept me voice neutral, asked,

"Yeah?"

"Oh yeah, Lucia, your partner's sister, she's regained con-
sciousness and I'm meeting her tomorrow, she might

be able to tell us who attacked her and if it wasn't that guy . . . Gino . . . ?"

I tried to stay calm, said,

"Wow, how about if I come along with you tomorrow, make it official?"

"That would be great, around nine o'clock . . . that suit you?"

"Perfect."

Click.

Fuck . . . fuck . . . Jesus, if she was able to talk . . . I swept the damn paper cup off me desk . . . I hate fucking vanilla . . . then began to calm down, hey, I'd the evening free, and man, I sure wanted another shot at her, and who knew, maybe the stuck-up nurse would be on duty, do her too . . .

I grabbed my jacket, ran into Rodriguez in the hall, who asked,

"What's up?"

I said,

"There's a mess in my office, get it cleaned up."

Come night, I go to the hospital, wearing doctor's scrubs, even a stethoscope, and fuck, I was so zoned, pure energy flying me on.

Found her room in jig time and there she was.

Radiant.

ONCE WERE COPS

In that half light they use in hospitals.

Her white neck . . . gleaming.

I pulled the blankets back.

Odd?

She looked fairly fucking comatose.

Probably the drugs.

What the fuck ever.

Snapped my medal off her neck and then got out the beads,
wrapped it round her gorgeous throat and then . . .
heard the sound of a gun being racked.

Turned to face Rodriguez, the fucking writer behind him,
and in the corridor a whole bunch of uniforms, he
said,

"Back away real slow, asshole."

I wasn't going to let the prick take me beads and moved to
get them and was slammed against the wall.

He shot me?

Me?

The blood was gurgling in my throat and I tried to say,

"But I'm a cop . . ."

The writer was staring at me with pure malevolence and
I wanted to tell him,

"I did the others but not Nora . . . I swear."

Heard Rodriguez say,

"The fuck is begging for help."

I didn't see any of them rush to get it.

The fuck is with that?

AFTER, AS JOE STOOD OUTSIDE, HIS EARS STILL RINGING from the gunshots, he was joined by Rodriguez. He stared at the cop, his anger barely controlled, asked,

"Why did you have to take him out?"

Rodriguez shook his head, said,

"You've forgotten what it's like to be a cop?"

Joe didn't get it, said,

"I don't get it, what's that got to do with you wasting him?"

Rodriguez faced him, his eyes a hard hue, said,

"The police department has enough bad press, you think we wanted Shea in a courtroom, *the hero cop*, on view to the whole world, best for all if he went down."

Joe wanted to wallop him, felt his fists curl, and before he could reply, Rodriguez said,

"I thought you'd be happy to see your sister's killer buy the farm?"

Joe took a deep breath, said,

"That was an execution."

Rodriguez turned to move away, said,

"No, it was expediency."

EPILOGUE

Joe was back in Miami a month now and couldn't settle, dammit all to hell, he had New York back in his blood, despite the cold, the traffic and all the usual stuff.

Plus, he couldn't get Maria off his mind, he'd given her his cell phone number and she promised to stay in touch. He was glad that his scenario about her might not be that far-fetched after all, just maybe she felt something too.

He was trying to put together a piece on all that had happened when his cell shrilled, he flipped the cover open, said,

"Yeah?"

"Joe, it's Maria."

God, he couldn't believe how happy he was to hear her but before he could say anything, she near screamed, barely containing her hysteria,

"Joe, *Dios mio*, one of the nurses has been strangled, the police say it is a copycat but he used a green rosary and last night when I got home, on my pillow was a gold ring, it had two hands holding a heart, I am so scared."

Joe, stunned for a minute, realizing it had to be Nora's ring, they'd never found it. He said,

"I'll be on the next flight."

She asked,

"But your job?"

He nearly smiled, said,

"Screw the job."